THE
MIDDLE AGES

EDWIN S. GROSVENOR

HORIZON • NEW WORD CITY

Published by New Word City LLC, 2016
www.NewWordCity.com

American Heritage Publishing
Edwin S. Grosvenor, President
P.O. Box 1488
Rockville, MD 20851

For more information about American Heritage, visit our website at
www.AmericanHeritage.com.

INTRODUCTION

It was during the Renaissance, which began in the fourteenth century, that the Middle Ages came to be thought of as the Dark Ages. It was a slander that would continue for the next five centuries. Inspired by the rediscovery of Greek and Roman writing on literature, philosophy, and science, the Italian scholar Petrarch divided history into three periods: the Classical, Middle, and contemporary eras. The Middle period referred to the millennium after the fall of Rome, and to Petrarch it was a time of ignorance and *Tenebrae*, or darkness. Other writers followed Petrarch's categorization, and the stain remained for the next 500 years. Finally, thankfully, reason returned, and historians have come to see the Middle Ages as a transition period from Late Antiquity to the Renaissance – a period of perpetuation, not destruction, of Roman culture. There were, of course, years of relative darkness, of rampant disease and warfare, but there were also interludes of radiant accomplishment.

Many of the modern historians who helped to reevaluate the Middle Ages wrote for *Horizon*, the extraordinary hardcover magazine published from 1958 to 1978. The essays from *Horizon* that are collected in this volume show that the Middle Ages were a time of struggle and triumph, folly and ambition, compassion and cruelty. For better and for worse, the events of the Middle Ages helped create the world we inhabit today. These pieces also make clear the interconnected nature of world events. Even in the

Middle Ages, when modern technology didn't exist, ideas traveled far and wide. Knowledge could not be contained. Unfortunately, neither could disease or other atrocities.

We set the stage in the opening chapter with a piece by Richard Winston about the Barbarians, who helped usher in the Middle Ages and the fall of Rome. The invasions could be brutal, but Winston also notes that the newcomers quickly adopted Roman customs. It was less about destruction than about control.

The history of the Middle Ages is one of overlapping events and struggles that lasted for centuries. A strict chronology doesn't give the necessary texture to the complexity of the times. So, these essays move back and forth across the sweep of the Middle Ages. There is a profile of the world of Charlemagne, who united much of Europe under his rule during the early ninth century. That's followed by an overview of Europe in the year 1000, an era once seen as the darkest of the Dark Ages, but perhaps also when the promise of dawn was being glimpsed.

Next is an exploration of Islamic rule in Spain during the Middle Ages, followed by a recounting of the Norman Conquest, a military invasion that in many ways helped create the United Kingdom as we know it.

From there, our story moves east, to the history of Byzantium, the empire created in the shadow of

Rome's fall. Once discounted as merely a spectacle of excess, Byzantium is now credited with having preserved much of what we now consider to be western culture. Then come two chapters about separate aspects of the Crusades. First, the highly personal war between Richard and Saladin for control of the Holy Land. Second, the rise of the Knights Templar, who embarked on a campaign of liberation in the Mideast only to run into a political firestorm at home in France. Following that is a profile of Alfonso, ruler of Spain after the fall of Islam there. He was a modern, nearly secular ruler, a compromiser and lover of the arts and science. Perhaps, not surprisingly, his reign was short-lived and disastrous.

Following Alfonso, we turn to the Troubadours, the songwriters and balladeers of the Middle Ages. More than mere entertainers, they also were satirists and broadcasters of an earlier era. Finally, we revisit the Black Death, the plague that ravaged Europe, killing a third of its citizens and having an impact on the continent for centuries.

What these pieces depict is an age that is neither dark nor the middle. Rather, what is clear is that it was part of the continuum of history, relentlessly pushing forward. The results can be unpredictable, not always pretty and not always displaying the full range of humanity. What the Middle Ages do reveal is that ambition and greed, optimism and hope, the love of literature and learning, and the desire for civilized society are not modern constructs. They are the building blocks of history and our collective lives.

1

THE BARBARIANS
RICHARD WINSTON

Goths, Huns, and Vandals: Were they savages who broke down the gates of the civilized world? Or was their notoriety the result of bad press?

Goths, Huns, and Vandals: Were they savages who broke down the gates of the civilized world? Or was their notoriety the result of bad press?

Barbarians. The word conjures visions of hordes of Germanic warriors ravaging the once flourishing cities of Gaul, Italy, and Spain, ushering in the Dark Ages. Then, so the story goes, the softening influence of Christianity shepherded these philistines to the milder habits of civilization, and then out of that jumble emerged medieval society.

The scenario fits into our preconceptions about sin, punishment, grace, and redemption, but it's a false doctrine. Yes, the barbarians helped bring about the fall of Rome, but the neat divisions of before and after belie a richer understanding of the barbarians and their own quest for what Rome had: the power to control its destiny.

Barbarians were not a race or ethnic group. They were more or less a political definition, signifying people who were not citizens of the Roman Empire. In that sense, they could be from anywhere on the map. Emerging from the central plains of Asia, the Huns encroached almost to Paris and deep into Italy. From Denmark, Germany, and Holland, the Angles, Saxons, and Jutes crossed the North Sea and took possession of England. The Eastern Germanic Burgundians seized the territory around Geneva as the Franks made their way into northern Gaul and remained there, giving the country of France its name.

Suevians and Vandals moved farther south into Spain, where the Suevians were assimilated into the population and the Vandals moved on to North Africa. Ostrogoths and Visigoths marched from Scandinavia to Italy (the Visigoths continued on to Spain); the Alans, nomads from Persia, traveled to the Strait of Gibraltar, and the Lombards crossed Germany into what is now Hungary and then moved into the part of Italy that today is known as Lombardy.

While certain groups of so-called savages did move into the Roman Empire between the fourth and sixth centuries, there weren't as many as earlier historians had suspected - no more than 80,000 Vandals, for example, crossed the Strait of Gibraltar into Africa, and fewer than half were warriors. Nevertheless, these intruders successfully established political factions within the empire - until the empire splintered.

With the exception of the Alans, Avars, Bulgars, Huns, and Magyars, the barbarians were of various Germanic groups, unaware of their shared language, race, and mutual culture.

The word "German," according to the first-century Roman historian Tacitus, was in his time comparatively new and had been extended from the name of a tribe to the whole people. Despite his many deficiencies, Tacitus remains one of the principal sources for our notions about the Germans of the pre-invasion period. In his historical account of the Germans, he describes them as a "distinct, unmixed race" of men with "fierce blue eyes, light hair, and huge frames fit only for sudden exertion."

Even though the Germans had entered into the Iron Age, Tacitus said, few used iron to forge swords or long lances - their primary weapon was a spear with a short, narrow head. They wore no armor, and only a few had metal or leather helmets. Their painted shields alone served them for defense. For the most part, the Germans obtained their weapons from the Romans through trade or by victory in battle; archaeological finds throughout Denmark, Germany, and the Baltic countries testify that the barbarians imported vast quantities of Roman arms.

These men wore furs - a simple cloak fastened by a clasp or a thorn. The wealthiest are distinguished by "a dress which is not flowing, like that of the Sarmatians and the Parthians, but is tight and exhibits each limb" - in other words, trousers. The women wore simple dresses of linen, often embroidered in purple with a revealing neckline.

Their diet was as simple as their clothing: wild fruit, fresh game, and curdled milk, along with beer and wine. Tacitus noted: "They satisfy their hunger without elaborate preparation and without delicacies. In quenching their thirst, they are not equally moderate. If you indulge their love of drinking by supplying them with as much as they desire, you can overcome them by their own vices as easily as by weapons."

Although overly fond of drinking and fighting, the

Germanic warriors operated under a fixed set of rules. They were less barbarian than we imagine. Their cultural hierarchy consisted of the nobility at the top, a middle class made up of free people, and slaves and serfs at the bottom. They had an organized religion and functioned under a limited form of democracy. There was no fixed bureaucracy or anything resembling a state in the grand tradition or style of Rome, much less a system of taxation. And unlike the essentially urban Romans, the Germans did not live in cities or towns nor did they congregate in large groups.

Greek historian Strabo noted that the Germans resembled the Gauls (whom Tacitus calls "effeminate") except they had lighter hair. Unearthed skeletons indicate that the Germans were not much taller than the Mediterranean people and certainly not a segregated group: As they migrated, they comingled with a variety of races.

In the years before the spread of Christianity in Europe, the religion of these early Germans centered on an elaborate mythology of gods and demigods. Like the Greeks, the Germans worshiped in sacred groves; like the Romans, they were highly superstitious; like the Hindus, they envisioned a cyclic universe in a constant state of flux of birth and decay.

As early as the second century, they had an alphabet and were familiar with writing, but rather than developing a literature, they used it primarily for magic and inscriptions. Their artisans were capable of inlaying silver into iron spearheads and producing beautiful gold filigree and were especially skilled in making jewelry and other ornamentation, such as silver chalices and elegant ceramics.

By the fourth century, when the "invasions" began, the Germanic nation, such as it was, had evolved into a more stabilized empire with fixed borders along the Danube and Rhine. They traded goods and slaves, had acquired a fondness for Roman luxuries, and had learned the uses and abuses of money. Some of this was not the result of trade. The Romans had incorporated entire tribes within their borders or formed alliances with others lying on the outskirts, taking hostages to ensure that treaties would be honored. As these hostages returned home, they brought with them a desire for education and a taste for Roman life. Slowly, the German world became more Romanized.

At the same time, there had been a "barbarization" of Roman society. With the institution of the *Constitutio Antoniana* in the third century, citizenship was granted to all free Romans living within the empire, reducing the necessity to enlist in the military as a way to earn citizenship. Now short of soldiers, the government enticed the barbarians to military service with offers of high pay, citizenship, and land. As the barbarians poured into the army, many rose to positions of power and prestige.

Romans soon began to mimic the barbarians. In the fourth and early fifth centuries, barbarian clothing and hairstyles became so popular that the Roman Emperor Honorius banned long hair and the wearing of fur coats - barbarian custom and costumes - in the cities of the empire. A greater indicator of barbarian influence was the rise to power of Stilicho the Vandal. This half-Germanic, half-Roman general, who had served as regent to the underage Honorius, was at one time the most powerful man in the empire. He served as consul, wed the emperor's daughter, and married his own daughter to the next emperor, all the while fighting wars against his fellow barbarians.

By the time Stilicho and Honorius, who became emperor at ten, had risen to power in the late fourth century, the Germanic barbarian "invasions" had already begun. But these invasions were not military incursions; rather, they were the consequences of Roman political maneuverings. Indeed, the barbarian "invasions" seem to prove, as so much history does, that statesmen can rarely predict the outcome of their policies.

The migrations began slowly. For centuries, Germanic tribes had been drifting southeastward into the steppes above the Black Sea, and by the third century, Goths and other tribes had left Scandinavia and moved into the Black Forest region near the mouths of the Danube. There, they lived alongside smaller bands of Germanic peoples and a larger group, the nomadic Alans.

According to Ammianus Marcellinus, a fourth-century Roman historian, the Alans were hunters rather than farmers; they ate meat and drank milk and lived in horse-drawn wagons with no place of fixed residence.

The Goths expanded the Alans' use of horses and wagons to bolster their military might, incorporating armor, long swords, and the lasso – a favorite weapon of mounted tribes. Despite differences in their language and culture, the Alans and Goths were so closely allied through politics and marriage that the Romans considered them one people.

At one time, the Goths controlled the territory extending from the Black Sea north and east to the Baltic and ruled over a variety of tribes. They even collected annual tributes from the Romans for guarding the frontier against less than friendly neighbors. During the third century, they persisted in raiding the empire, but in times of peace, provided soldiers for Roman armies. The year 332 ushered in a long period of peace, during which Ulfilas, a bishop and missionary who translated portions of the Bible into Gothic, converted many of his fellow Goths to Christianity. It was a shaky conversion. Ulfilas was an Arian belonging to a sect that did not believe in the Holy Trinity, slowly poisoning the Goths' relationships with the Catholics of the Roman Empire.

There were soon to be other disruptions, chiefly the

sudden onslaught of the Huns. In their migration from the eastern Asiatic region - likely Mongolia - the Huns had assimilated a number of nomadic tribes into their army. Their strange habits evoked terror in Europeans. These warriors practiced cranial deformation - the deliberate flattening of the heads of their children - along with euthanasia of the elderly and cremation of their dead. They seemed to live in the saddle, allegedly ate their meat raw, rarely or never washed, and fought with unspeakable savagery. They are described as small in stature, with broad chests, disproportionately large heads, tiny eyes, and flattened noses.

The sudden invasion of the Huns in 374 and 375 shattered the Gothic and Alanic kingdom of the Ukraine. The Gothic king committed suicide; his successor was killed in battle. A portion of the Ostrogoths, the eastern branch of the Goths, surrendered to the Huns and became their allies while the rest of them - the western Visigoths, the majority of the Alans, and other terrified tribes, pleaded with the Roman emperor Valens for permission to cross the Danube.

Reluctantly, Valens consented, and the Goths settled in Thrace (comprising parts of modern-day Bulgaria, Greece, and Turkey), where the Romans capitalized on their desperate situation, charging such exorbitant prices for bread and meat that the Visigoths revolted. On August 9, 378, at Adrianople, the Visigoths killed Valens and decimated the Roman army.

After their triumphant victory, however, the Visigoths did not know how to consolidate their power. They tried and failed to capture Constantinople, then gave up and made peace with Theodosius, the new emperor of the Eastern Roman Empire, who took them on as mercenaries; when Theodosius attempted to reduce their pay, they rebelled once again. Alaric, a Gothic soldier frustrated by his failure to advance in the Roman army, led the Visigoths on a fifteen-year campaign through Illyria, northern Italy, and Greece that ultimately arrived in Rome. The only Roman general who could keep the Visigoths in check, either by bribes or force, was Stilicho the Vandal. But he was assassinated in 408, and Rome was doomed. In August 410, Alaric's Goths sacked the city.

This event was not a haphazard one. For years, Alaric had negotiated with the Romans for peace. When it was not forthcoming, his patience ran out, and on August 24, 410, his men forced open the Salerian Gate and entered Rome. Alaric gave his soldiers permission to plunder the city but not to kill anyone unless the person was armed and to respect the sanctity of the churches. The Goths were so remarkably restrained that later Roman writers extolled their good behavior.

With the news that Rome had fallen for the first time in 800 years, shock reverberated throughout the Roman world. In response to the pagans' assertion that Rome had been punished for abandoning its gods and embracing Christianity, Saint Augustine began writing his treatise, *The City of God*.

After the conquest of Rome, Alaric and his men set out to invade North Africa, but upon reaching the Strait of Messina at the southern tip of Italy, their fleet was destroyed by a storm. To compound the disaster, Alaric died suddenly, probably of disease. For his burial site, the Goths diverted the Busento River near the town of Cosenza and had their prisoners dig a grave for their young king in the old riverbed.

Alaric's men buried gold, silver, and weapons with his body and then allowed the river to revert into its old channel. According to Jordanes, a Goth historian, the soldiers killed their prisoners to preserve the secret of the burial place.

Once Alaric was dead, his successor, Ataulf agreed to enter negotiations with the western Roman emperor Honorius, who pressed the Visigoths into service once more and sent them to Spain, to defend against the Vandals, and into southern Gaul, where they fought against the Huns. The Visigoths in Gaul were eventually expelled by the Franks, but the Visigoths in Spain converted to Catholicism in 587 and merged with the people of Spain. Goths continued to reign until the Arab invasion destroyed their kingdom in 711.

The Goths had originally been sent to Spain to fight the Vandals, who were similar to the Goths in many respects. The Vandals spoke a Germanic dialect akin to Gothic and may have been neighbors of the Goths in Scandinavia. As they moved southward, they situated themselves west of the Goths, then moved even farther west toward the Roman fortifications on the Rhine. When Roman troops were withdrawn from the Rhine to combat Alaric's soldiers, the Vandals crossed into Gaul accompanied by Burgundians, Suevians, and other Germans.

Next, the Vandals entered Spain. Driven from the Pyrenees by the Visigoths, they held their ground in southern Spain until the combined forces of the Visigoths and Roman Spaniards pushed them out; once ousted, they moved on to North Africa. Forbidden by the Romans to build ships, the Vandals nevertheless seized fishing vessels, built ships of their own, and in 429, sailed across the Strait of Gibraltar to Tangier. Unable to defend North Africa, the Romans instead offered to ally themselves with the barbarians. Gaiseric, the Vandal king, accepted, and within ten years, built an independent Vandal state with a sizeable navy that inhibited Roman commerce.

In the middle of the fifth century, at the invitation of a faction in Rome, the Vandals invaded Italy. In 455, like Alaric, they sacked Rome, but at the request of Pope Leo the Great, abstained from destroying the city and satisfied themselves with pillaging, doing little to justify their modern reputation for wanton destruction.

As a matter of fact, the word "vandalism" seems to have been used first in the eighteenth century by the bishop of Blois, who compared the destruction caused by the Jacobins in the French Revolution to the supposed crimes of the Vandals 1,400 years before.

The Vandals adapted quickly to Roman civilization. In North Africa, they adopted Latin as their language and took pleasure in the Roman customs of baths and spectacles. Within two generations, they were displaying an interest in literature and even theology. But their kingdom collapsed in 533 when Belisarius, Emperor Justinian's great general, invaded North Africa. Two weeks after landing, Belisarius captured Carthage; within a year, all traces of Vandal rule had been obliterated. The Vandal nation vanished from history, leaving behind only a bad - albeit unjustified - reputation.

The Huns likewise did not warrant their reputation as barbarians and implacable enemies of civilization. After destroying the Gothic kingdom in the Ukraine, they settled in the region north of the Danube and enjoyed fairly good relations with the Roman Empire. The peace ended, however, when Attila became king in 434 and terrorized the Balkans for the next fifteen years. Then, in 450, just as the Vandals were attacking Italy - Attila invaded Gaul. Shrewdly, he negotiated with the Franks and received an offer of marriage from Honoria, the sister of Emperor Valentinian III, who had made Attila his *magister militum* - master of the soldiers.

Attila's march into Gaul was checked by Flavius Aetius, a Roman general who had aligned himself with the Visigoth king Theodoric I to stop the Hun invasion. At the Battle of the Catalaunian Plains, after staggering losses on both sides, the combined Romano-Gothic forces defeated the Huns yet failed to capture Attila, who withdrew with his remaining troops. What was left of Attila's army was still strong enough to invade Italy a year later, but disease and hunger soon forced the Huns to retreat.

The following year, 453, Attila died. His followers placed his body on a bier in a silken tent in the middle of an open field, and in accordance with ancient traditions, celebrated the funeral rites of their king. When the revelry ended, they buried Attila in a three-layered coffin made of gold, silver, and iron and filled his grave with precious gems and armor taken from vanquished enemies. To protect the grave from robbers, they killed the workmen who had taken part in the burial.

Attila's sons, squabbling with each other over their inheritance, soon lost control of their subjects, who rose up in rebellion, marking the end of the Hun Empire.

The greatest barbarian migration, however, was that

of the Ostrogoths in Italy. Split in half by the on-slaught of the Huns, one group of Ostrogoths fought with Attila in Gaul and Italy. After his death, they allied under a king named Valamir and defeated the Huns in a decisive battle. On the day of that victory in 455, a son was born to Valamir's brother. He was named Theoderic, meaning "ruler of the people," and he was destined to become just that.

After some skirmishes with the Romans, Valamir and his Goths were hired - for 300 pounds of gold a year - to guard the borders of the empire. To ensure that they would maintain the peace, the king's neph-ew, Theoderic, by then eight years old, was taken to Constantinople as a hostage, where he became a fa-vorite of Emperor Leo and was educated by the Ro-mans and taught the techniques of Roman govern-ment and military tactics. At eighteen, he returned home to his father, Theodemir, who had succeeded Valamir on the throne.

Their time together was brief. Theodemir died in 474, and Theoderic became king of the Ostrogoths, who were now residing in Macedonia. When the emperor Zeno was expelled from Constantinople by a rebellion, Theoderic supported his return to of-fice and was rewarded with the rank, privileges, and compensation of commanding general in the impe-rial army. In addition, Zeno adopted him as his son, potentially giving Theoderic claim to the imperial throne.

In spite of this, Theoderic's relationship with Zeno was fraught with tensions. As Theodoric grew in stature, the emperor began to regard him as a dangerous rival, and rightly so; the young tactician was successfully gathering around himself the scattered Gothic troops of the Eastern Empire. In 488, after Theoderic's troops blockaded Constantinople, Zeno got rid of him by sending him to Italy to evict the German usurper, Odoacer, who had deposed Romulus Augustulus, the last Roman Emperor of the West, twelve years earlier.

While Theodoric and his multi-national army conquered the peninsula of Italy quickly, Odoacer holed up in the nearly impregnable city of Ravenna, on Italy's northern Adriatic coast, in a siege that lasted four years. To end the impasse, Odoacer offered to share his kingdom with the Roman-Ostrogoth alliance. Theoderic honored the agreement for exactly ten days. On the ides of March 493, he invited his co-regent to a palace feast and assassinated him.

After this unsavory beginning, Theoderic ruled Italy as a benevolent despot for thirty-three years, the longest period of peace and prosperity the country had known for centuries. He sought out competent men to fill high offices, fostered literature and learning, and reestablished the commerce of Italy. He was tolerant of his Catholic subjects, as well as pagans and Jews. But his passion was construction. Palaces, baths, churches, and theaters rose in Rome, Ravenna, Verona, and many smaller cities.

Throughout his reign, Theoderic maintained an outwardly subservient relationship with the Roman emperor in Constantinople, but in actuality, they operated as equals. While he called himself king, he was not the king of the Goths - or Germans, or Romans – but simply *Flavius Theodericus rex*. His influence extended far beyond the boundaries of Italy; at times, he was the recognized leader of the West. Still, he accepted his legal inferiority to the legitimate emperor in Constantinople and was content with the official position as Master of the Soldiers for Italy.

After Theodoric's death, Justinian, the last Latin-speaking emperor of the East, undermined his work and finally doomed the Western Empire. Justinian tried to recapture the lands the empire had lost in Western Europe, a task his general, Belisarius, had easily accomplished in North Africa. But it took twenty years of desperate fighting before the imperial forces finally defeated the Gothic armies. Italy never recovered. Instead, it fell prey to a new group of barbarians - the Lombards, who had begun their warring and wandering centuries earlier in what is now southern Scandinavia. Even less civilized than the Goths, they still drank from cups made from the skulls of their enemies. Lacking the organizational talents of the Goths, they splintered Italy into numerous petty duchies.

The movement of the Lombards into Italy was not the last of the great migrations. The Lombards were followed by Avars, the Avars by Magyars and Turks and various Slavic tribes. Then from the north came the Vikings. The Celts expelled from England by the Saxons invaded what is now Brittany.

By the end of the sixth century, the great Roman Empire had ceased to exist. In Britain - now merely a network of Anglo-Saxon kingdoms - the Latin language and Roman influences had nearly vanished. Spain continued to be dominated by Visigothic kings. In Italy, the Lombards were gaining ground. The pope acquired administrative powers in Rome and its surrounding territories, becoming the *de facto* ruler long before the Papal States were created by Charlemagne's father, Pepin the Short.

Central Gaul and part of what is now Switzerland were held by the Burgundians. In northern Gaul, Clovis I had united all of the Frankish tribes, establishing the Merovingian dynasty, which would rule the kingdom for the next two centuries. Once the Franks had established a power base in Roman territory, they pushed into Germany, civilizing the barbarians to the east. The barbarian rulers were securing their revenues to maintain their empire from vast personal estates, but they also organized a makeshift military government to replace the elaborate Roman bureaucracy. The era of a strong central government would not be restored until the advent of the Carolingians in the ninth century.

Gradually, the Roman educational system and Roman law were abandoned. In Aquitaine, Italy, and North Africa, schools for the private sector continued to exist, but the quality of education declined. In other parts of Europe, the Church assumed the responsibility, leading to a vastly different system of education.

The emergence of medieval civilization from that of the Romans is a complex subject. Ultimately, of course, the entire quality of life changed. But in the period of the last barbarian invasions and immediately afterward, such medieval phenomena as chivalry, Scholasticism, and Gothic cathedrals still lay far in the future. Despite the political upheavals, many aspects of life remained unchanged, especially in the southern part of Western Europe.

Christians were inclined to interpret the chaos of the times as a sign that the last days were coming. Thus, Saint Ambrose could write, "We are, indeed, in the twilight of this world." Nevertheless, the emperor in Constantinople was still the emperor. The popes acknowledged their subservience to him even though they were becoming virtually independent. The chanceries of barbarian kings continued to date documents by the reigns of the emperors in Constantinople. Throughout Western Europe, the literate continued to write in Latin, and Latin remained the language of the common people. Only in England was there a violent rupture with tradition, and only there did a barbarian vernacular take the place of Latin.

Perhaps the greatest consequence of the barbarian migrations was the destruction of the Roman aqueducts; after Theoderic's reign, no new aqueducts were built, nor were the old ones repaired. The most significant destruction took place in Rome itself, where in the middle of the sixth century, the Goths besieging Belisarius cut the great aqueducts, leading the patricians to abandon their palaces on the hills and come to the banks of the Tiber, drawing their water from the river or wells. Torrents of water from the broken aqueducts poured out over the plains of the Campagna, transforming wheat fields into malarial swamps.

The cities of the empire were already shrinking because of the decline of commerce, the displacements of political power, and the ravages of disease. The bubonic plague of 542-543 reduced the population of Europe by 25 million. The lack of water was the final blow. And as the cities died of thirst, medieval rustication began.

With the end of the empire, the Western world returned to agrarianism. That was partially the result of barbarian influence - many of the barbarians feared the walled towns of the Romans. "A walled enclosure seemed to them a net in which men were caught, and the city itself a town to bury them alive," Ammianus Marcellinus commented. But the resurgence of agrarian life was primarily a result of complex economic and political forces that originated in the empire itself - the insecurity of life, the slowing of trade, the destruction of the middle class, the breakdown of central government, the shift from a money economy to a natural economy, and so on. Europe returned to the soil. It would be centuries before a new cycle of urbanization could begin. When towns again sprang up, the barbarians - now only barbarian in name - built the institutions that linked medieval urban society with the modern world.

2

THE AGE OF CHARLEMAGNE
RÉGINE PERNOUD

In the history of Western civilization, few men have had as profound and lasting an influence on the court of human events as Charlemagne, who, as king of the Franks, united a huge swath of Europe under his rule.

In the history of Western civilization, few men have had as profound and lasting an influence on the court of human events as Charlemagne, who, as king of the Franks, united a huge swath of Europe under his rule.

In the history of the Western world, three men have at separate times held sway over most of the European continent - Caesar, Charlemagne, and Napoleon. Of the three, it may be argued, Charlemagne has had the most profound and lasting influence on the course of human events. The great historian Lord James Bryce, writing in 1864, had no doubt about it. The coronation of Charlemagne as the first Holy Roman Emperor on Christmas day in the year 800 was, to quote from Bryce's own rich prose, "one of those very few events of which, taking them singly, it may be said that if they had not happened, the history of the world would have been different." It was from that moment, when Charlemagne was acclaimed emperor, wrote Bryce, that modern history began.

Those large statements serve to remind us that the historical importance of Charlemagne's reign was far greater than its material achievements. Within a few generations after his death in 814, the empire he had so laboriously pieced together was already in shambles. In his later years, the aging emperor is said to have wept at the thought of the menacing advances of the Vikings along the northern and western fringes of his realm. Now, ever more boldly, the dreaded longboats with their high dragon prows were slipping up the Seine, the Loire, and other waterways, spreading terror and destroying every vestige of imperial authority wherever their raids reached. Paris itself was sacked in 845. In 846, Saracens from northern Africa, raiding from the south of Italy, attacked Rome and violated Saint Peter's and the tombs of the Apostles. Then nomadic hordes of Magyars, from the area now encompassed by Hungary, pressed in to ravage the eastern borders of the empire. And in the meantime, Charlemagne's heirs and descendants were incapable of maintaining any semblance of political unity within their crumbling borders. Once again, Europe divided into a dismal miscellany of contending and often hostile forces.

Yet, the great emperor had left an indelible mark. It was in the generations of dissolution following his death that legends of grandeur started to cluster around his memory. He was described as "the Emperor with the Flowery Beard," gigantic in size and 200 years old, held in awe from Britain to Baghdad as the invincible Christian conqueror. He was credited with miraculous prowess and implausible virtue. According to some chronicles, he would rise from the dead to vanquish the enemies of his realm; according to others, he did, in fact, so rise to take part in the Crusades. He soon became the center of an epic cycle of romance - best remembered in the *Chanson de Roland* (*Song of Roland*) - that spread enchantment throughout the Middle Ages and down the centuries to our own day. In 1165, he was even transformed into a saint by the antipope Paschal III, and the day of Saint Charlemagne, the "inventor of schools," was a cherished holiday for the school children of France until the twentieth century.

However extravagant their growth, the legends about Charlemagne were rooted in historical realities, although they often have an epic quality that challenges the imagination.

Charlemagne was a man of immense energy and strength, a superb horseman and an accomplished swimmer. His wives, mistresses, and concubines were numerous, but his amorous indulgences did not interfere with affairs of state or war. He was immensely curious, many-sided in his interests, and demanding of those from whom he could learn. Although no verifiable portrait of him has survived, he obviously had a commanding presence. The force of his personal influence gave shape and direction to the trends of his age and to future events.

The greatest achievement of that era was, in effect, nothing less than the founding of Europe - that is to say, the welding of the fresh vigor and energy of the Teutonic north to the civilized traditions of the Roman south in the name of the Christian faith. Geographically speaking, Europe is not a natural unity; it is rather a physically disparate extension of Asia. But out of the fusion of what is known as the Carolingian period evolved a common European consciousness that, in spite of constant tensions and intermittent bloody ordeals over the centuries since, continues to assert itself. It was in this new Europe, as Belgian historian Henri Pirenne has remarked, that Western civilization evolved and expanded to become that of the whole world. And nothing reveals the greatness of Charlemagne more clearly than the zeal with which this almost unlettered warrior attended, supervised, and encouraged the birth of the new culture. Viewed in historical perspective, his coronation marked the consolidation of this achievement. The ceremony changed nothing in fact, but it did give formal recognition to Charlemagne as the Christian emperor in the West and a rival of the Byzantine emperor in the East.

It is also true that many of Charlemagne's accomplishments had been initiated by others. Indeed, the foundations upon which he built so splendidly had been laid long before his birth. Nevertheless, the year 732 marks a sharp turning point in the destinies of the Frankish state, a point to which the ascendancy of Charlemagne can be directly traced. It was in this year that Charles Martel, grandfather of the emperor-to-be, checked the advance of Arab invaders at a great battle near Poitiers. This crucial encounter took place precisely one century after the death of Muhammad, and in the course of that 100 years, his militant followers had overrun Asia and Africa from the Indian Ocean to the Atlantic, gaining recruits as they progressed. They had crossed into Spain and conquered the kingdom of the Visigoths, and, aid-ed by large hordes of converted Berbers from North Africa, they had then swarmed over the Pyrenees.

The fear provoked by their deep penetration into what is now France was real and desperate; the shock of relief that followed their repulse reverberated down the years to come. It was in the wake of this repulse that the line of Charles Martel in the person of his son Pepin, father of Charlemagne, was established to rule the Franks.

More than two centuries before, the Franks forged the first true European state to take shape from the general wreckage that followed the invasion of barbarian tribes and the fall of Rome. With the conversion of their great ruler, Clovis, about 496, and the attendant mass conversion of his followers, the Franks became the stalwart champions of Roman Catholicism north of the Alps. To this large, central area newly opened to the faith streamed emissaries from papal Rome, and even more important, monks and missionaries from England and Ireland. The latter included the most learned and devout men of the time, and at a point when Continental civilization had all but vanished, their work among the Franks and among the heathen beyond the frontiers helped to lay the foundations of a new age.

It is claimed that the greatest of all these Anglo-Saxon pilgrims, Saint Boniface of Crediton, had a deeper influence on the history of Europe than any other Englishman who has ever lived. He founded the

German Church and sowed the seeds of a new cultural life. And when the Merovingian line of Clovis had degenerated beyond any hope of resuscitation, he anointed Pepin with sacral oil and named him king of the Franks.

A few years later, Pope Stephen II, with great travail, crossed the Alps and journeyed north to the abbey church of Saint Denis where he personally anointed Pepin afresh - and for good measure, Pepin's two sons, Charles (the future Charlemagne, then twelve years old) and Carloman. He not only anointed them kings of the Franks but proclaimed them "Patricians of the Romans," a title that, in effect, made them protectors of Rome. In several campaigns, Pepin established papal authority over territory that had been usurped by the Lombards - thus laying the foundation of the Papal State, which endured for more than a millennium, and at the same time, marking the beginning of the imperial mission of the Carolingians as leaders and organizers of Western Christendom. That the lands thus disposed of were the legitimate possessions of the emperor at Constantinople did not in any way impede the transaction.

Before his death in 768, Pepin had, by and large, succeeded in consolidating his Frankish kingdom. The territorial aggression of the Lombards in Italy had been thwarted, and Pepin had placed the northern part of the peninsula under his own protection. The Arab invaders had been driven out of France altogether, and Pepin had added to his realm their earlier holdings in the southwest as well as the nearby duchy of Aquitaine. To the east, Bavaria acknowledged his authority, and the Saxons had been contained along the northern frontier. When, upon the death of his brother and co-heir in 771, Charlemagne, now twenty-nine, became sole king of the Franks, he was already the strongest ruler in Western Europe.

For the next thirty-odd years, by almost incessant warfare, Charlemagne strengthened and amplified his position until his dominions stretched from the Mediterranean and northern Spain to the North Sea and from the Atlantic to the Elbe and the lower Danube, uniting most of the lands that are now France, western Germany, Austria, Switzerland, Liechtenstein, the Netherlands, Belgium, Luxembourg, and a good half of Italy. He quickly and finally destroyed the power of the Lombards and assumed, for his own purposes, the iron crown of that kingdom and all its wealth. In successive, bloody campaigns, he virtually obliterated the Avars, the mounted nomads from the Eurasian steppes who had been the scourge of Eastern Europe and who had laid siege to Constantinople. And he plundered from their treasure such riches as the Franks had never seen before. Charlemagne generously shared this fabulous loot with his faithful courtiers and servants, the abbots and bishops of his kingdom, the pope, and even King Offa of Mercia, self-styled monarch of all the English.

The most celebrated of all Charlemagne's campaigns

and the most famous of all medieval wars was his ill-fated expedition in 778 against the Muslims who controlled Spain. Although he had recruited a formidable "international" army, including warriors from all parts of his realm, and had been promised the support of Spanish collaborators, Charlemagne was unable to win a decisive victory, and he soon retreated across the Pyrenees. Here it was - in the mountain pass of Roncesvalles - that the Frankish rearguard was cut to pieces by a guerrilla band of Christian Basques.

Both before and after that debacle, it required eighteen separate campaigns to subdue the Saxons and to force them to baptism in the Christian faith. In the course of one of these, 4,500 men were beheaded in a single day, and a third of the rebellious population was resettled in distant places. "After he had thus taken vengeance," the annals calmly recite, "the king went into winter camp at Thionville and there celebrated Christmas and Easter as usual." Although his spiritual advisers reminded him that such butchery and deprivation were not the most persuasive methods of conversion, to Charlemagne these were wars of religion; as the anointed leader of Roman Catholic Christians, he fought with the sword for the cross. "It is my duty," Charlemagne reminded Pope Leo III - who was later to crown the emperor - "with the help of divine piety, to defend the Holy Church of Christ with arms on the outside against the raids of pagans and the ravages of the unfaithful, and within to protect it by diffusion of the Catholic faith. It is your duty, very holy Father, lifting your hands towards God with Moses, to help the success of our arms with your prayers." In another letter, the king indirectly but emphatically admonished the pope "to live honestly and to give special attention to observing the holy canons," and in all ways to run an incorruptible, exemplary office. Charlemagne presided over his kingdom of God on earth with all the theocratic powers of the ancient Hebrew kings; indeed, among his intimates, he chose to be addressed as David.

To those looking for more recent parallels, he seemed the re-embodiment of Roman imperial authority. More than eight centuries had passed since Julius Caesar had conquered Gaul, and more than three centuries had passed since the last Caesar of the West had given over to the remote Eastern emperor at Constantinople the dominion of the European Roman world. But the conviction that the Roman Empire of Caesar and Augustus had never ceased to exist faded slowly. That empire, as one historian has observed, seemed to be "a necessary mode of being of the world, above the accidents of historical facts." For all its despotism, it had established peace and order, to which men's minds turned with stubborn nostalgia throughout the long, convulsive period of the barbarian invasions. And in spite of the violence and cruelty with which Charlemagne imposed his sway over Europe, people were beginning to sense again the blessings of the *Pax Romana*.

In 799, violence broke out in Rome, and Pope Leo was assaulted on the city's streets. The pope already had sent Charlemagne the keys to the grave of Saint Peter and the standard of the Eternal City and had pledged his loyalty and obedience to his Frankish protector. Now, he fled north to beseech the king for his aid. Charlemagne crossed the Alps again, restored order in Rome, and reestablished the papal authority and dignity. It was during this interval, in 800, while Christmas Day Mass was being celebrated, that the grateful pope crowned Charlemagne with the diadem of the Caesars. He had become, as the crowds acclaimed him, "Charles Augustus, crowned by God, the great and peace-giving Emperor of the Romans." It is not known whether this ceremony was planned in advance and with Charlemagne's approval. It did not matter. The crown fit securely, and in time, even the emperors of the East acknowledged as much.

Charlemagne did not revive the Roman Empire except in name. At his coronation as emperor, he wore the Roman long tunic and cloak, but it is significant that he never dressed that way again and never returned to Rome after this visit. In spite of his consuming interest in the revival, preservation, and dissemination of classical culture, which gave his reign the character of an early medieval renaissance, Charlemagne always remained a Frank. He chose as a new and permanent capital the old watering town of Aachen between the Rhine and the Meuse, on the western border of present-day Germany, an area with which his Carolingian forebears had long been associated. And here he built a splendid palace with a church that seemed to his contemporaries a structure "half human, half divine."

For untold centuries, the Mediterranean had been the maternal, nourishing element of all intellectual vigor and of all creative spirit. Urban life at Alexandria, Athens, Constantinople, and Rome had fed the growth of all civilizing tendencies and developments from ancient history. Now the center of cultural ferment, in Europe at least, had shifted to the heartland of the rural dominions of the Franks - to a land that a few centuries earlier had been identified with long nights, dark forests, and crude barbarism. But out of this north were generated those influences that strongly conditioned the growth of a new European society.

The administration of Charlemagne's sprawling empire was a highly personal operation. Through his inheritance and by his conquests, peoples of many varied tribal traditions – Bavarians, Burgundians, Franks, Lombards, and Saxons, among others, not to mention Romans - had been brought within the imperial jurisdiction. He did not attempt to abolish their customary laws, but he had these committed to writing and then proceeded to refine them and add to them a voluminous flow of capitularies, or ordinances, of his own, which were final and beyond appeal.

To be sure that these promulgations were observed throughout the land, Charlemagne dispatched pairs of royal emissaries called *missi dominici,* or envoys of the lord. Usually consisting of one secular representative and one cleric, they were responsible directly to the emperor. They checked periodically in the most intimate detail on the behavior of his subjects - from the efficiency of high public officials to the sex habits of the lowliest monks. The welfare of his subjects rested almost completely in his own two hands. He was, as a contemporary phrase stated, "Lord and Father, King and Priest, the Leader and Guide of all Christians." And it may be fairly said that no one with such great power has abused it less.

Nothing better illustrates Charlemagne's vision of his "universal" state and of his own responsibility, under God, for its welfare than his determination to raise the educational standards of his people and restore for their benefit the neglected knowledge of the past. The seed of such a revival had already been planted by Boniface and his fellow missionaries a generation or two earlier. Now, forced by the enthusiasm of the king, it came to flower during his lifetime. There was no more eager student in the realm than Charlemagne himself. Charlemagne had a well-informed if not brilliant mind, but he never mastered the art of writing, although he "used to carry with him and keep under the pillow of his couch tablets and writing sheets that he might in his spare moments accustom himself to the formation of letters." He was intellectually curious, and he gathered about him the brightest and most competent minds of the time. The old palace school of earlier kings was transformed into an academy of distinguished theologians and scholars who were enlisted from all parts of the realm and beyond.

The intellectual excitement that Charlemagne instigated by his recruitment of learned men, centered in the palace school, was to spread throughout his empire, largely by way of the monastic and episcopal centers of the land. Indeed, in an agrarian world, the great Carolingian abbeys such as Tours, St. Gall, Reichenau, Fulda, Lorsch, Corbie, and others became the creative sources of civilization, as cities had been and would be. They were the basic social and economic centers of the age, and within their precincts were developed those traditions of art and letters, of architecture and liturgy, of music and calligraphy, which were to remain the essential cultural endowment of the centuries to come. They survived the emperor's death and the political chaos that followed. Indeed, in later years, King Alfred of England sent to the Franks for scholars who could help in the re-education of his country. It can be claimed that in providing for the needs of his rude Christian society, Charlemagne laid the foundation of all modern education.

As one single example of this lasting influence, this page is printed in letters derived from the calligraphy developed in Carolingian manuscripts, called the Carolingian minuscule, a style of writing that became standard in most of Western Europe. More than 90 percent of the oldest, surviving, classical Latin texts were made in this style. For a long time, these were mistakenly considered to be Roman manuscripts, and the characters themselves still are called Roman letters.

In arts and architecture, as in letters, Charlemagne hoped to invigorate his northern world with a return to the forms and traditions of the earlier Roman Empire. The design of his palace chapel at Aachen, which provided a model for many other Carolingian churches, was based on the church of San Vitale at Ravenna. To complete this structure, he purloined classical columns, bronze gratings, and other ancient elements from Italy. In the end, it was not an imitation of any older model but a vigorous northern interpretation, a creative fusion that served to stimulate the development of new architectural styles and concepts.

The murals, mosaics, and sculptured reliefs that adorned such Carolingian structures have, along with the buildings themselves, almost entirely disappeared. It is in the so-called minor arts - ivories, metalwork, and particularly, illuminated manuscripts - that the spirit of the age is most revealed to us (illumination denotes drawings and other decorations in the margins and borders). The most characteristic feature of Carolingian illumination is its tendency to return to the classical tradition, particularly in its renewed interest in the representation of the human figure. Yet neither the Roman occupation of earlier centuries nor the classical revival of Charlemagne's time destroyed the rich cultural traditions of the Celtic, Germanic, and other "barbarian" people who had migrated across Western Europe. For barbarism is not savagery but rather a degree or stage of social organization; it is a tribal culture rather than one of a settled, authoritarian state. These people brought with them a heritage in their arts as in their folkways that was deeply rooted in a distant past and in part inherited from the Sarmatians, Scythians, and other eastern tribes with whom they had come in contact during their earlier migrations.

Charlemagne recalled from threatened obscurity the ancient traditions of art, as he had salvaged from possible destruction classical manuscripts of enduring importance. The "renaissance" he had fostered gained momentum, attaining an even more complete development in the generation following his death in 814. Some of the finest manuscript illuminations were created during the reign of his grandson, Charles the Bald. But in his efforts to revive the ideals of classical antiquity, as is so often the case in such "revivals," Charlemagne merely performed the last rites over the past; and as is also often the case, he signaled the advent of something new and different.

By an old, established, and highly misleading convention, the term Middle Ages has been applied to that long period between the fall of Rome and the beginning of the Renaissance, as though the medieval world was simply a way station between antiquity and modern times. By an even more unfortunate convention, that millennium has been broadly labeled the Dark Ages - implying a time of intellectual and cultural stagnation. Actually, it was a period of assimilation, ferment, and consolidation. There were, indeed, years of relative darkness, but there were also interludes of radiant accomplishment. None of these had greater import for the future of Western civilization than the age of Charlemagne.

3

EUROPE IN THE YEAR 1000
MORRIS BISHOP

A millennium ago, our forebears lived in a "Dark Age."
They themselves did not think it was dark, and
they were only half wrong.

A millennium ago, our forebears lived in a "Dark Age." They themselves did not think it was dark, and they were only half wrong.

Let us fix our gaze on the state of Western Europe over a millennium ago in CE 1000. What was our world like? And what were its inhabitants, the forbearers of many of us, like?

Look first to the east to the Russian steppes. There, the Slavs dwelt and pushed ever westward. Their flourishing towns, Kiev and Novgorod, rivaled the best in Western Europe. The Bulgarians moved into their Bulgaria. The Poles thrust out of Russia to their present home, where, in 966, their duke, Mieszko, was baptized a Roman Catholic, and all his people, by his order, were converted overnight. The Hungarians, a people from beyond the Urals, appeared in the West at the end of the ninth century. They ravaged and looted as far as Burgundy, but defeated by the German Otto the Great in 955, they settled down in their new homeland and became peaceful farmers and devout Roman Catholics. Theirs was the last serious barbarian invasion of Europe, for the rampaging fourteenth-century Turks were hardly barbarians. Henceforth the barbarous foe was to come not from beyond eastern borders but from underneath.

Constantinople was the capital of the Eastern Empire, a centralized state with an efficient standing army, a competent bureaucracy, subsidized schools and hospitals, a sophisticated art and literature fostered by the Orthodox Eastern Church. A Western envoy to Constantinople in 949 was bedazzled by the emperor, richly jeweled, sitting on a golden throne beside a bronze tree with twittering bronze-gilt birds. He was guarded by gigantic lions. His throne could be elevated on high like a garage lift.

Islam ruled from India to Spain, but by the tenth century, it lost its expansive impetus and settled down to the enjoyment of its culture and gracious living. In Spain, under the Ommiad dynasty, living could be gracious, indeed. The land was irrigated and bloomed like a garden, yielding rice, sugarcane, cotton, citrus fruits, as well as wheat and olives. Innumerable workshops produced arms, leather and silk goods, carpets, textiles, and pottery for export as far as China. The capital, Córdoba, boasted a half-million residents, 700 mosques, many Christian churches and Jewish synagogues, 300 public baths, a 400,000-volume library, and a university with courses in mathematics, astronomy, theology, philosophy, medicine, and law. At the time, there were no universities in Latin Christendom.

Arab physicians were famed throughout the West. Poets and poetesses abounded. Their romantic love songs, with their cult of the inaccessible lady, deeply affected the later Provençal troubadours, and through them, our modern conventions of wooing in verse and music. The Arabs were passionate sportsmen, delighting in archery, polo, horse racing, hunting, hawking, tennis, and croquet. They delighted, too, in festive parties with singers and abundant wine. (The wine was, of course, prohibited by law, but there was no lack of Christian and Jewish bootleggers.)

By comparison, the Christian West was mostly wild country, repossessed by the dark forest, the home of wolves, bears, wild boars, and aurochs, the ancestor of domestic cattle. It also was the home of outlaws and robbers and of gnomes and goblins guarding once-sacred trees and springs. Here and there were the marks of abandoned cultivation, hummocks hiding forgotten towns and lost cities, the dwellings of evil pagan ghosts.

The Roman remains - the broken aqueducts and overgrown amphitheaters - seemed the work of giants. Old Roman roads marched unswerving over hill and dale, but roots and bushes pried their stones apart, and many of the old stone-arched bridges had fallen into the streams. The inhabitants were unconcerned; the broken highways discouraged invaders. Overhanging it all was a sense of ruin, of descent from a greater and happier past. Here was the Dark Age, as modern historians, in their misplaced pride, termed it.

In 909, a Church synod reported with sober justice: "The towns are depopulated, the monasteries ruined and burned, the good land converted into desert. Just as primitive men lived without rule and without the fear of God, subject only to their own passions, so today everyone does what he pleases, in scorn of human and divine laws and the commandments of the church. The strong oppress the weak; the world is filled with violence toward the defenseless, and men pillage the church's property. Men devour one another like the fishes of the sea."

True enough, but it is always darkest before the dawn. By 973, matters had improved. The savage Vikings had been bought off by the grant of Normandy as a homeland, and they, like the Hungarians, came to prefer farming to plunder and Christian doctrine to the service of bloodthirsty gods. Arab pirates still roved the Mediterranean; they were established on the French Riviera. From Alpine passes, one of which is still known as Monte Moro, they raided northward, attacking even the Swiss monastery of Saint Gall in 954. In the year 972, they took captive and held for enormous ransom the Abbot of Cluny as he was crossing the pass of Great Saint Bernard out of Italy. This indignity provoked the count of Provence to wipe out the pirate nests and drive the Arabs back across the sea.

There were other alleviations in life in the tenth-century world. Few plagues and epidemics are reported. Neglected land was brought back into cultivation; new agricultural techniques improved the yield of thin, exhausted fields. The population grew with an increase in food production but at a faster rate. Research by Professor Lynn White of the University of

California at Los Angeles attributed the increases to a new profusion of proteins in the form of broad beans, peas, chickpeas, and lentils. There were similar population explosions in China, the Mideast, and the Scandinavian north.

The Western world of 1000 was fragmented, a bundle of localisms. England, to be sure, enjoyed a brief cohesion under Edgar the Pacific (959-975). But Edgar died young, and troubles aplenty awaited his successors, including Ethelred the Unready, or the Stupid.

France was a collection of baronies and dukedoms, mutually hostile, united chiefly by opposition to their king. The nominal king of France was Lothair, next-to-last of the line of Charlemagne; he ruled precariously over Paris and the Île-de-France.

Italy was a power vacuum. The north was a congeries of nearly independent city-states, imperial fiefs, and bishoprics wielding temporal rule. Rome and the surrounding Papal States were the property of the Church. Calabria and Apulia, the heel and the tip of the boot, belonged to the Eastern Empire in Constantinople. Sicily was under Islamic rule.

Only in Germany was there something approaching national unity, under Otto I. Duke of the Saxons and king of the East Franks, he checked the invading Hungarians, Slavs, and Danes, fostered the Christian faith, and made an alliance with Byzantium. In 962, he revived the Roman Empire, with himself as emperor. In 973, his son Otto II became emperor. But the empire was hollow; it had no imperial administration and little control over the mighty dukes, barons, and prelates of Germany.

A good share of the fragmented world was precariously ordered by the social-governmental-economic system of feudalism. The word itself has unfairly been tarred with ugly connotations. The feudal system arose in response to needs - the need of the poor for protection and the need of the strong for soldiers and for upkeep of their strength. Feudalism was a bargain. The poor exchanged freedom for security, for they would rather be safe than free, and anyway, freedom meant little when there was no place to go and nothing to do when one got there.

Feudalism had its elevated doctrine, its ethos of loyalty, courage, and honor. The feudal lord was not necessarily an oppressor. The system was at its best a workable one, based on land and the land's products, not on money. If serfs were bound to the land, the land was bound to them; they could not be dispossessed and driven into an unwelcoming world. Feudalism encouraged a certain peace of mind. Every person's status was fixed, his or her destiny and duties clear.

Of course, the feudal ideal was open to dreadful abuse. Force could readily usurp right. A brutal lord could rob, torture, and kill his serfs without offending his overlord or his conscience. He could go to war with his neighbors at will, to adjust a boundary, claim a daughter's or a wife's dowry, avenge a slight to his honor, or merely to beguile boredom.

The tenth-century economy was not a market economy like our own. Gold and silver coins were seldom seen, but a sheep, a chicken, an egg had visible value. Life was centered in the village, a kind of cooperative for the exploitation of land. The village clustered about the log-built stronghold of the feudal lord, with its flour mill, forge, bakery, and chapel. The village was also a social unit, a club for the organization of country dances and religious celebrations. The village bought little from outside - salt, pig iron for the smith, needles, fishhooks, and such. It had nothing much to sell, except farm surplus, and often none of that. Transport was costly and difficult, market fairs rare and widely scattered.

Nevertheless, some villages were growing into market towns, and some centers - such as London, Paris, and the Rhineland cities - lingered from the Roman past. These were walled and often moated; though the inhabitants crowded together, they prudently left room for gardens, crofts, and food storage. The townsmen supported a garrison and an abundance of clerics, for the town became naturally an administrative center for the Church. Some craftsmen were at work, making armor, cloth or candles. And more and more merchants were appearing.

We don't know a lot about trade and commerce in

the tenth century. Luxury goods such as silk and spices filtered in from the East - but the only purchasers were nobles and churchmen. In return, the West supplied metals, furs, some foods, especially salt fish and English cheese, and French wine, and slaves. The merchants were the bold, the hardy, the clever - often ex-serfs - who ventured, and frequently lost, their lives on the perilous roads.

Much of the Western world was unquestioningly Catholic, although the Church sanctified relics of pagan practice and for many, the concept of faith was but a mere bargain with the saints for preservation and salvation. The papacy set the worst of examples; it underwent a moral slump not to be matched until the coming of the Borgias. Election to the papal throne was controlled by a clique of Roman nobles and the infamous Marozia, mistress of one pope, mother of another, grandmother of a third. Of her grandson John XII, it was written: "His rapes of virgins and widows had deterred the female pilgrims from visiting the tomb of St. Peter, lest, in the devout act, they should be violated by his successor."

Benedict VI was elected in 973 and strangled the next year, under the direction of Marozia's sister. Papal turpitude did not, however, infect the great structure of the Church. At a council of French bishops in 991, the Bishop of Orléans would dare to characterize the papal regime as the coming of Antichrist.

The bishops were mighty men. As feudal lords, administrators of colossal estates (in Germany as much as a third of the territory), they wielded temporal as well as spiritual power, and they ruled as well as, or better than, their noble peers. If nothing else, they were much less likely to go to war.

The spiritual life centered on the monasteries. Some of these, to be sure, settled into a comfortable routine, with a minimum of mortification of the flesh. The monks of Farfa, near Rome, when summoned to reform, rebelled and poisoned their abbot. Even Saint Benedict's own Monte Cassino was relaxed. It is said that a certain Calabrian zealot made a pilgrimage there. Under its walls, he heard the sound of a guitar from within and was informed that the monks took regular baths. Shuddering, he returned to his hermitage.

It's instructive to look at two of the monasteries. First is Saint Gall in Switzerland, founded in the seventh century, and the home of a long line of learned and virtuous men. It was self-contained and self-sufficient, with barns and stables, a threshing floor, a grist mill, an orchard, and a row of workshops for craftsmen. A hostel served wayfarers; an infirmary with a resident physician cared for the sick.

At Saint Gall, learning was prized and encouraged; both sacred and profane texts - even those in Greek - were beautifully copied. Two schools were operated - an inner school for novices and oblates, monks in the making, and an outer school for youths who were to remain in the world. Discipline was strict, but holidays were celebrated with games, races, shot-putting, and at day's end, a common bath and wine feast by torchlight.

Cluny was quite different. This was a reform monastery, founded in 910, in protest against the relaxations and abuses within the Benedictine rule. Here the *Opus Dei*, the service of God by prayer and praise, was almost continuous. It was presumed that in recompense for Cluny's unending chants and austerities, God might pardon the sinful world.

The monks ate bread, vegetables, fish, and a little cheese. In the scriptorium, the monks copied only sacred texts. If they had need to consult a heathen book, they indicated the fact by scratching their ears "as dogs are wont to do, for it is not unjust to liken a heathen to such an animal." The Cluny reform was widespread; eventually, it was accepted by 1,450 houses. Clearly, it answered a need for deeper piety, for self-sacrifice, for immolation to an ideal.

The world of 1000 had these centers of devotion and of learning, islands in an ocean of ignorance. Most of the identifiable structures of the period were abbeys with their churches. These followed in form the traditions of the Roman, and Carolingian, basilicas, but the choirs were enlarged to accommodate the singers and clerics, and ambulatories were added to provide for processions and for chapels dedicated to saints, with their relics. Frescoes and mosaics adorned the walls; the good Bishop Adalbéron of Reims invented storytelling windows of colored glass. Stone roof-vaulting was attempted, to replace wood. Particularly in Germany, ambitious prelates built imposing structures, including those at Augsburg, Magdeburg, Mainz, and Cologne. Their style has been called Ottonian, or Pre-Romanesque, or First Romanesque.

The church supported a wide range of arts. Sculptors carved birds and beasts on the tops of columns. Craftsmen made jeweled reliquaries, processional crosses, candelabras, chalices; they fired enamels and cloisonné ware, and delicately embroidered vestments. Most notable was the art of bookmaking - calligraphy and illustration. In England, the Winchester School developed a representational style, with line drawings of men and women engaged in everyday activities.

It was a largely barren period for creative literature, but more artful productions were in formation. The Irish and Slavs already had their epic poems, composed and sung by minstrels. Latin hymns, rhymed and accented, evidently inspired vernacular imitations; so, too, did Arabic lyrics migrating into Provence. Simple men, in moments of emotion, made up simple songs about love, or springtime, or tragic death - as they do today. But no one thought of these popular songs as literature. "The vernacular is good enough for the devil," said an abbot of Saint Gall.

At the same time, the drama was coming to a fumbling self-consciousness. The Easter liturgy was commonly acted out, with monks and responsive choirs taking the roles of angels and holy women at the Resurrection. And there was the surprising case of Hrotsvitha, a nun of Gandersheim in what is now Central Germany, who wrote six Latin comedies in the style of the second century BCE playwright Terence, with saints and miracles as the subject.

Medieval men and women were irrepressible singers, for group song is a form of communion. At the feasts of the early Anglo-Saxons, the harp passed from hand to hand, and every man sang and played in his turn. For the first time, the bowed fiddle appeared. Musical notation was invented, to indicate pitch and duration. The addition of a second voice inspired the later development of polyphony.

Science, as we know it, did not exist. The idea of experiment and discovery did not fit with the concept of a fixed creation, ordained from on high. However, agricultural technology improved markedly, and in medicine, there were some stirrings of scientific spirit. A researcher has found fifteen medical handbooks dating from the tenth century. In the monasteries, a cleric, showing aptitude, was deputized to use leeches and treated his comrades with herbs and bloodletting, which were believed to harmonize the humors and reduce the passions. Surgery was relatively advanced. Broken limbs were reset, or, if gangrene appeared, amputated. We are told of plastic surgery for harelips and the use of urinalysis.

It is said that a duke in Bavaria tried to befool Abbot Notker Balbulus of Saint Gall by sending him, as his own, the urine of a pregnant woman. Notker announced: "God is about to bring to pass an unheard-of event. Within thirty days the Duke will give birth to a child." Of course, the service of physicians was restricted to the rich and noble. Common folk sought help from wise women and witches who practiced folk medicine. The poor patients were probably no worse off than the rich.

Such, glimpsed in snapshots, was the Western world of a thousand years ago.

The mark of their minds was faith, a great comfort. There were as yet few heretics and fewer rationalizing skeptics. The simple man made no distinction between natural and supernatural; the supernatural was natural. A miracle was an everyday occurrence. Reproduction and growth, winter storm and springtime bloom, the body's recovery from illness, seemed miraculous, and very properly, too. Evil spirits had their hellish home only a few yards underfoot; their visits to earth were well attested. The chronicler Raoul Glaber said he saw the Devil several times. Once by his bedside, Satan was a little black monster in human shape. Fortunately, the angels overhead were just as close, able to watch our acts and swoop down to rescue us from deserved disasters. We may have been insignificant little people on this earth, but saints and angels loved us, and we loved them.

Life was short. Productive years even shorter. Menaces abounded: famine, polluted water, and tainted meat, infections of ill-tended wounds, and raging diseases, such as malaria, typhoid, diphtheria, dysentery, tetanus, puerperal fever. Infant mortality was high; hence, women were expected to marry at puberty and begin having babies, a hazardous process. They had to produce perhaps three times as many offspring as today, just to keep the population stable.

Death was commonplace in every household. Perhaps its familiar presence encouraged a prevailing callousness or brutality. Monarchs set the example, with their blindings and removals of hands, testicles, ears, and noses. Mutilation was a common penalty; malefactors could seldom pay fines and there were no prisons for their confinement. People regarded suffering as inevitable, indeed rather amusing. The comic misadventures of the blind and the lame were a favorite subject for medieval stories. Of course, it was understood that a patient sufferer expiated his own sins and those of others.

Nature itself was equally cruel. Beyond death and disease were floods and drought and Arctic blasts. In the northern winters, men hugged the fire in a drowsy and probably malodorous torpor. We have few reports of medieval smells; even the delicate gentry did not notice them. Men lived with their animals and bathed only in summer. Clothing was handed down from generation to generation; there was no dry cleaning and only an ineffective soft soap. Darkness, especially in the north, curtailed activity. Glass was a luxury, and the householder's windows were shuttered against the cold. Indoors, resinous torches or rank-smelling tallow candles cast a feeble gleam, so that women could spin and men whittle spoons, shape farm tools, or weave baskets. Then the storyteller or the ballad singer came into his own.

Food varied with the region and with class. One could map all of Europe with divisions into wine regions, beer regions, cider regions, with a special patch for then-Muslim Spain. Or one could divide the world into butter lands and olive-oil lands.

The class difference in foods was equally well-defined. The noble ate meat, game, and pastries; he was punished for vitamin insufficiency by skin diseases, a furious springtime itch, and occasional scurvy. The peasant had little meat, usually only in the autumn when the scrawnier pigs and cattle were slaughtered to save winter feed. Their product was certain to be tough; a favorite joke was to refuse the meat and ask for a piece of hide. Herring and other fish were plentiful near the coasts. The peasant's staples were vegetables, especially peas, beans, lentils, cabbages, turnips, leeks, and onions, and bread, whether of rye, barley, oats, or wheat.

The important meal came in the evening after the day's work, and the main dish everywhere was a great stew, the contents being everything available. Honey and fruit were the only sweeteners. Except in bad years, the peasant's food was abundant, though unvarying.

As for housing, our noble ancestors of the tenth century occupied crude wooden strongholds. Except in Germany, there was little in the way of masonry or stone-cutting and the lime and cement to make mortar were hard to obtain. The noble family, with their retainers, dwelt together in the hall or common room, by night unrolling their straw pallets on the floor. The peasant cottages were built of whatever materials lay at hand. In England, they were chiefly wattle-and-daub. Upright stakes were "wattled," or intertwined with shoots and twigs, and "daubs," or dabs, of clay and mud were plastered on. A poorly daubed house could nearly dissolve in a downpour.

The roofs were tile or shingle, or thatched straw, an efficient rain-shedder but verminous. A hole in the roof served as a chimney. The floor was of hard-packed mud, and like adobe, could be surprisingly durable. But it also froze up and thawed with the seasons and was one good rain away from returning to its original state. Rheumatism was a constant threat. The poorer families crowded into a single room together with their farm animals and poultry.

The furnishings were scanty - perhaps a table, benches or stools, a chest, wooden bowls, mugs, and spoons, sometimes a bedstead. Earthenware cooking pots were common. There were no glass mirrors. They owned no more than enough to provide shelter, warmth, clothing, and food, and even that little was sometimes begrudged them. An English abbot told his serfs they owned nothing but their bellies.

Were they happy? The question is perhaps an idle one. The people of the time did not ask it, or at least, they have given us no answer. Their lives were given to labor, but it was mostly labor in common in the open fields, and except at plowing and harvest time, it was not unduly burdensome. A village was small indeed, but it was big enough for social life, for frolics and games and dances, for courtship and exciting rivalries and triumphs. The village was the villager's whole cosmos. He was not aware of anything farther away than the end of a half-day's walk. Beyond lay a world more mysterious than heaven and hell. In his village, his home, he was incurious and probably content.

We need not pity overmuch our forefathers and foremothers of 1000. They were fulfilling their destiny, humankind's destiny, preserving the seed of the future, our seed. What if their age looks to be a dark one, in the long roll of ages? In that dark, the Western world was stirring, preparing the birth of modern civilization. "If the age was dark," said Lynn White memorably: "its darkness was that of the womb.

4

WHEN MOORS RULED SPAIN
GERALD BRENAN

Less than 100 years after they had hurled themselves
out of the desert, Arabs were building in Spain a civilization
that lasted almost 800 years and cast a bright ray of
light into the Dark Ages of Europe.

Less than 100 years after they had hurled themselves out of the desert, Arabs were building in Spain a civilization that lasted almost 800 years and cast a bright ray of light into the Dark Ages of Europe.

One morning in July 711, a battle took place that decided the fate of Spain for more than five centuries. The country, except the sliver in the Pyrenees, was then ruled by Visigoths, who had occupied it during the last years of the Roman Empire. But far away in the East, a new power had arisen which, under the inspiration of a prophet called Muhammad, had overrun Egypt, Mesopotamia, Persia, and Syria. Exhilarated by their easy conquests, the armies of this new religion had marched on along the African coast till they reached Morocco. Here they had orders to stop, but the attraction of slaves and booty was too strong: Tarik, the military governor of Tangier, sent 400 men across the Straits of Gibraltar to see what could be picked up. They returned with a cargo of beautiful women who so impressed Musa ibn Nusair, the caliph's governor in North Africa, that he ordered Tarik to take across a stronger contingent the following year.

Tarik landed with a small force, while Rodrigo, the Visigothic king, marched to encounter him with a much larger one. They met on the banks of the shallow lagoon of La Janda, close to Tarifa at the southern tip of Spain, and Rodrigo was defeated. Musa himself landed the next summer with another army, and within a couple of years, most of the Iberian

Peninsula was occupied by the invaders.

The ramshackle but oppressive Visigothic regime had fallen, and a much more vital one had taken its place. Over the course of years, the Muslims were to introduce into Spain the culture of the Alexandrian Greeks and the refinement of the Persians, creating a brilliant civilization that could compare with anything in the East. When Muslim rule ended, the Christian state that emerged after centuries of fighting was, as one might expect, a militant state fortified by a militant church. The Spaniards acquired the special character they have had since the Middle Ages not so much by learning from the Moors as by crusading against them, and the culture they eventually adopted was borrowed in all but a few details from France and Italy.

At first, however, the Muslim invaders had it entirely their own way. Across Spain, they were greeted with open arms. This was partly the result of their tolerant and easygoing policy: Everyone who submitted was allowed to keep his estates; the privileges of the great feudal lords were confirmed by special treaties; and there was religious toleration, except that Christians had to pay a poll tax from which the Muslims were exempted. So many Spaniards went over to the new faith in order to escape taxation that within 100 years of the Arab conquest, most of the population professed to be Muslim.

Yet at first, the Muslims did not bring settled government. For forty years, the country was torn by civil strife. The old feuds of the desert broke out again on Spanish soil, with the men of northern Arabia lined up against those of Yemen. A raid into France to loot the tomb of Saint Martin of Tours was repelled by Charles Martel in 732 at Poitiers, marking the farthest limit of the Muslim advance. At the same time, a center of Christian resistance appeared in the mountains of Asturias, in northwest Spain. The Visigoth chieftain Pelayo, hiding in a cave with his thirty followers, marks the beginning of the Reconquista. Soon his successor, Alfonso, was carving out a kingdom in the wet, forested country, which held no appeal for the Muslims. From now on, there were to be two Spains, perpetually at war with each other.

Meanwhile, great changes were taking place in the East. The Umayyad caliphate of Damascus had been undermined by the rise of the Shiite and Kharijite branches of Islam, and in 750, it fell and was succeeded by that of the Abbasids at Baghdad. The new caliph caught and beheaded every male member of the Umayyad family except one. This was Abd al-Rahman, who escaped to Morocco. From there, on the invitation of one of the factions, he crossed to Spain in 755 and the next year was proclaimed emir of al-Andalus, as the Muslims called their Spanish kingdom. He was twenty-five, and his real difficulties were only beginning.

Abd al-Rahman reigned for thirty-two years. Every one of those years was filled with risings and insurrections, made not by the conquered Spaniards but by his ungovernable compatriots. Even his own family conspired against him, and he needed all his energy and ruthlessness to maintain his position. He was a sad man who always dressed in white, the color of his house, and his private tastes lay in gardens and plants which, with the nostalgia of the exile, he imported from his native Syria. But we owe him a debt of gratitude for building the Great Mosque at Córdoba. It was the finest Arab mosque of the time and marked a breach with all previous styles of building. Art progresses by having new problems to solve, and in this case, the difficulty to be overcome lay in the shortness of the old Roman columns he had decided to re-use. The roof needed to be much higher, so above the columns, the architect designed a double tier of horseshoe arches; this in turn led to another discovery, the intersecting arch. Most of the original features of Spanish Arab architecture derive from this innovation.

Abd al-Rahman was succeeded by his son, Hisham I. His short reign (788-796) was notable for the introduction of the conservative Maliki school of theology, and in Spain, it became more conservative than anywhere else. Under the direction of the *fakihs*, or men of religion, it led to an intellectual paralysis that until the end of the caliphate (in 1027) prevented any discussion on philosophic or scientific questions. Every work on these subjects was regarded as heretical. Since the Muslim world elsewhere was being racked at this time by religious controversies, the Maliki orthodoxy helped to keep Spain quiet, and so it was supported by the emirs. It is reminiscent of the rigid doctrinal control exercised later by the Spanish Inquisition in order to keep out Protestantism.

The next two emirs had very different reigns. The first, al-Hakam I, was a pleasure-loving man who enjoyed hunting cranes by the river, playing ball, and listening to recitations of poetry; but he incurred the enmity of the *fakihs* because he drank wine, and they stirred up against him riots and rebellions that he put down with great severity. This allowed a long and peaceful reign (822-852) to his successor, Abd al-Rahman II. The work of consolidation now seemed to be over, and the emirate of Córdoba took its place among the leading states of the world. It had few rivals. The Abbasid caliphate in Baghdad was in rapid decay, North Africa had split up into independent states, and Europe was sunk in the lowest depths of the Dark Ages.

In contrast to this, the life of the court and aristocracy at Córdoba was one of refinement and luxury. Exquisite brocades, gold and ivory caskets, rare books, and accomplished singing girls were imported from the East.

The person who taught the Córdoban court and aristocracy how to display wealth with elegance was the Iraqi musician Ziryab. He was the best singer of his day and is said to have known more than 1,000 songs by heart. He invented a lute that had five strings instead of four and set up a conservatory where "Andalusian" music, still heard today in the gardens of Fez, acquired its form. But he was more than a musician; he was a man of culture and taste. Finding the customs of the Córdobans crude and provincial, he decided to reform them. With the encouragement of the emir, he laid down rules as to what clothes should be worn in each season, how hair should be styled, and how food should be cooked and served. Thus we find him introducing asparagus and substituting drinking glasses for goblets and replacing tablecloths of stamped leather with damask ones.

The Muslim states had a predictable rhythm: a generation or two of stable government followed by a period of chaos, with discontent due to bad trade or crop failure being fanned by local disaffection or religious fanaticism. So now, after Abd al-Rahman II's death in 852, thirty years of utter anarchy set in. The mountainous region of the south rose under a guerrilla leader from Ronda, and all the great cities rebelled and declared themselves independent. The emirate of Córdoba seemed about to disappear when, in 912, a young man of twenty-one succeeded to the throne. This was Abd al-Rahman III, who was perhaps the greatest ruler Spain was ever to know.

It took him twenty years of hard fighting to impose his will on the country. After that, he had to contain the Christian states of the north and to assert himself in Morocco, which had been conquered by the Fatimid dynasty that ruled in North Africa and Egypt. It was not till 929 that he felt strong enough to take the next step and assume the title of caliph, Commander of the Faithful. This was possible because the caliphate at Baghdad had by now sunk to a shadow.

Córdoba at this time was a city of well over half a million inhabitants. It was a place of great wealth, and its Muslim aristocracy, hidden away in their palaces and gardens, lived in ease and luxury. In addition to the Great Mosque, which had now been enlarged, there were 700 smaller mosques and oratories and 900 public baths. But the court was the center of everything, and to get an idea of it, one must look at the new palace that Abd al-Rahman III built a few miles outside the city. Medina Azahara he called it, according to legend, after a harem favorite. It took thirteen years to build because it was not only a palace but an administrative center that had to house a considerable population. The palace apartments contained 14,000 male domestics, all of them Franks, and 6,000 women, including slaves, living in the harem. As an indication of the cost of supplying this establishment, we are told that 12,000 loaves of bread were brought in every day merely to feed the fish in the ponds. The decoration was as lavish as anything to be seen at that time in Constantinople or Baghdad. Four thousand marble columns lined the mosque and the various arcades, while the walls of the principal apartments were decorated with green and rose marble imported from Tunisia. The ceilings were gilded and the doors inlaid with silver, ivory, and precious stones. But the room known as the Hall of the Caliphs surpassed all the rest. Its vaulted ceiling was encrusted with mosaics, its windows were of translucent alabaster, and it was entered by eight doors paneled with glass. In the center, there was a huge marble basin filled with quicksilver. A mechanical device enabled a slave to agitate it, making the whole room appear to be turning in circles and throwing out spokes of light.

It was in this hall that Abd al-Rahman received the embassies of foreign nations. One came from Emperor Otto of Germany and another from the Byzantine emperor, Constantine Porphyrogenitus (literally, to the purple-born). To reach the caliph, they had to ride for four miles between rows of armed and mounted soldiers and then pass on foot through room after room spread with rare Oriental carpets and hung with silk brocades. At the end, they saw the caliph seated on his throne, with his eight sons and his viziers and chamberlains standing on either side of him, and looking, as Otto's ambassador wrote, like an inaccessible divinity. On another occasion, old Queen Tota, her son King Garcia of Navarre, and her grandson Sancho the Fat, deposed king of León, arrived and prostrated themselves before him. The caliph had sent Sancho a doctor to cure him of his fatness, and now that he was thin again, he had come to beg for an army to restore him to his throne.

It can be imagined what an effect these receptions had on the poor monarchs and ambassadors from the north. Europe was now touching its lowest level of misery and squalor, so that to a German or a Basque, the court of Córdoba must have been dazzling. Yet it should be remembered that everything the caliphate could show - ceremonies, institutions, objects of luxury and display, palaces, libraries - had been borrowed from Damascus or Baghdad. There had been a complete break with the Roman and Visigothic world, and except for the architecture of the Great Mosque, nothing new in the arts and refinements of life had made its appearance. A cultivated Iraqi or Egyptian would have found Córdoba dull and provincial.

However, there was one outlier to the Oriental color of al-Andalus, and that lay in the language. The upper classes spoke most readily the debased Latin, mixed with Arabic words, that was growing into Spanish. The emirs and caliphs learned it in the nursery since their mothers, like most of the women in the harem, were Galician or Basque. For this reason, many of the caliphs had blue eyes and fair hair.

Abd al-Rahman III died in 961 after a forty-nine-year reign. He was a man of great presence and majesty who surrounded himself with Byzantine ceremony yet was frank and easy with his friends. His generosity and benevolence made him well-liked, and he had achieved all he had set out to do. Yet it seems he was not content. After his death, a paper was found on which he had noted those days of his reign when he had been completely happy and free from care. They numbered only fourteen.

His son al-Hakam II was forty-six when he succeeded to the throne. He was a bookish man of poor health with a loud voice, a beaked nose, and short legs. He had spent the years before his succession in assembling and reading from a library of 400,000 volumes. Few libraries in Europe at this time contained more than 500, but the manufacture of paper had recently been introduced from China to Iraq and paper books cost only a fraction of those made from vellum. Many private persons in Córdoba also acquired large libraries; the standard of education in the city was so high that almost everyone could read and write at a time when, in northern Europe, few princes or emperors could read a line.

Al-Hakam II's reign showed a steady advance both in literary culture and in the luxury crafts: gold and silver, ivory and silk, leather work. It no longer relied on the East for these products. In agriculture, new plants were introduced, including rice, sugar-cane, cotton, the date palm, and the pomegranate. (Sweet oranges and lemons came in later.) Mulberry trees were planted in great numbers to feed the silkworms, and the area of land under irrigation was greatly extended, transforming the plains of Valencia, Granada, and Málaga into verdant oases. In the cities, gardens were laid out with roses, Madonna lilies, and sweet-smelling herbs, edged with borders of rosemary or boxwoods. In northern Europe, the formal garden had not yet seen the sun.

After a reign of fifteen years, al-Hakam II died in 976, leaving a child of twelve, Hisham II, to succeed him. The real ruler, however, was not to be Hisham but an ambitious court official, Ibn Abi Amir, best known by the title he later took: al-Mansur, "the Victorious," which in Spanish became Almanzor. By seducing Hisham's Basque mother, he was able to raise himself to the position of chief minister. Then, to conciliate the *fakihs*, he ordered all the books in al-Hakam II's library that discussed science or philosophy to be destroyed. Finally, to secure the army, he married the daughter of the powerful frontier general, Ghalib. But the critical moment of Hisham's coming of age was approaching. Fortunately for Almanzor, the young caliph was a weak creature who had been brought up in the harem and was alleged to be unnaturally preoccupied with sexual indulgence. He was therefore easily persuaded to delegate the management of public affairs to his chief minister on the grounds that he wished to give himself up to religious exercises. So after suppressing an uprising by Ghalib, Almanzor became the sole power in the country.

His first act was to give orders that his name should be mentioned immediately after the caliph's in the mosques. This gave him the treatment of emir. He then married a daughter of the Christian king of Navarre, who paid him a visit in Córdoba, prostrated himself humbly, and kissed his feet. Ten years later, Almanzor took a third wife, a daughter of the king of León. Meanwhile, he had built himself a new palace and chancellery just outside Córdoba. Paraphrasing the name of Abd al-Rahman III's palace, he called it Madinat al-Zahira, "the brilliant city," and all the offices of the government were housed there. The older palace-city then became almost deserted.

But it is as a military commander, "the Scourge of the Christians," that Almanzor acquired his reputation. He began by reorganizing the army, increasing the number of the Berber and Frankish mercenaries, and reducing the strength of the native Andalusian levies. Then he pacified Morocco, extending his influence as far as the city of Fez. He was now free to give all his attention to the Christian states in the north of Spain. Twice every year, he led an army of from 30,000 to 60,000 men across the frontier, capturing and sacking cities, cutting down trees, and bringing back as slaves the inhabitants he caught. Barcelona, León, Coimbra, Zamora, and Burgos were all taken by him, then burned and destroyed. But Almanzor's crowning exploit was his raid on the shrine of Saint James at Santiago de Compostela. After Rome, it was the most famous pilgrimage place in Europe, and Almanzor knew that its destruction would send a wave of terror and anger through the Christian world. Marching northward along the Portuguese coast so that his fleet could provision him, he reached the city without opposition and found it abandoned. He demolished it thoroughly but spared the tomb of Saint James and the solitary monk who stood guard. Then, carrying with him the doors and the bells of the basilica, he returned to Córdoba. Five years later he was dead. A monk of Burgos recorded it tersely in his chronicle: "In 1002 Almanzor died and was buried in Hell."

These enormously expensive expeditions that the caliphs and Almanzor led across the Christian frontier were not aimed at conquest. No attempt was made to gain and occupy fresh territory. They were simply raids, made in fulfillment of the command of the Prophet to carry on a holy war against the infidel. They had also the secondary purposes of raising the prestige of the ruler and of capturing slaves. The raids were violent affairs. Battlefield prisoners were executed. Cities were burned. Regular citizens were taken into slavery.

But that violence belied a fundamental transactional relationship between the two sides.

In al-Andalus itself, complete religious toleration prevailed, and Muslims and Christians intermarried freely. There was some trade across the frontiers, conducted by Jews, and the people of the north imitated the manners and dress of the Muslims. Most surprising, the kings of León and Navarre sometimes enlisted the help of Muslim armies in their civil wars, while in Almanzor's raid on Santiago, we read of a number of Leónese counts helping him assault the holy shrine. Religion to the men of that day was one thing; war with the profit and honor it brought was another.

Almanzor was succeeded in power by his eldest son, who died after a reign of only six years, and then pandemonium broke out. During this period, the feeble caliph-in-name-only, Hisham II, was forced to abdicate; a great-grandson of Abd al-Rahman III replaced him as caliph; and contending factions sacked and demolished, within a few months of each other, first the Medina Azahara and then the Madinat al-Zahra. The latter was the work of rebellious Berber mercenaries who marched back from the frontier and, after destroying al-Zahra, laid siege to the city. At the end of a year and a half, it was starved into submission and the Berber troops poured in, looting the palaces and killing the inhabitants. But the Berbers had no wish to remain in Córdoba. The caliphate was finished, so they obliged the puppet whom they had put on the throne to cede to them the provinces of Granada and Jaén. Other Berbers from Africa occupied Málaga and the surrounding hill country; Frankish mercenaries took the east coast from Almería to Valencia; and the Muslim governors of Seville, Badajoz, Toledo, and Saragossa each proclaimed their independence. Córdoba settled down to be a republic, ruled by its Arab aristocracy, and the twenty years of anarchy known as the *jitna* were over.

Muslim Spain had now broken up into some thirty

independent states, and it would be understandable if the high standard of culture and learning which had developed during the caliphate declined. In fact, the opposite happened. The Taifa kingdoms, as they were called, saw a flowering of literature and science. For the rulers of these new states, always in competition with one another, culture was an article of prestige. They lavished their money on libraries and *objets d'art* and on salaries to poets, philosophers, and mathematicians. The *fakihs*, who had lost much of their influence, had to bow to this. Thus, while the states where the Berbers had settled remained backward, Seville, Córdoba, Almería, Toledo, Badajoz, and Saragossa became centers of art and science.

Poetry had always been the chief art form of the Arabs, even in the days before Muhammad. The caliphs of Córdoba had not only written poems themselves but had maintained a body of professional poets at their court (Almanzor is said never to have gone on a campaign without taking at least forty with him). But this poetry had often been of poor quality. Now, a number of eminent poets appeared whose work could compare with anything that was being written in Byzantium. There was, for example, Ibn Hazm, a Córdoban of Spanish descent who also wrote a remarkable prose work on the psychology of love, as well as a comparative history of religion. This was the period in which Provençal poetry was springing up in the south of France. The idea that writing love poetry was a proper occupation for courts probably emanated from al-Andalus, and with the poems, perhaps, came a certain new attitude toward women. One of the causes of the ending of the Dark Ages was the discovery that the Muslim countries possessed a more refined and luxurious style of living than northern Europe and the desire of the feudal lords to raise more money so as to emulate it.

The Taifa kingdoms lasted a bare sixty years. They were too weak to hold back the advancing Christians. Unwillingly, therefore, they called in the new power that had arisen in Morocco. Known as the Almoravids, these camel-riding Berbers from the Sahara lived on dates and veiled their faces (as their descendants, the Tuaregs, still do). They were recent converts to Islam, full of zeal and fanaticism. Their emir, Yusuf, landed in Spain, cut to pieces the Castilian army that had marched to meet him, and then took control of the Taifa kingdoms, tightening their spendthrift ways. The poets had to stop writing because there was no one to pay them their pensions, and the philosophers had to go into exile because the *fakihs* hated them. After the death of Yusuf in 1106, there was a little more latitude, but Spanish Muslim culture was now looking to the past rather than the future. When Ferdinand III of Castile captured Córdoba in 1236 and Seville in 1248, Muslim rule in al-Andalus was over. Only the small kingdom of Granada remained.

But back in 1084, just before the Almoravids crossed over into Spain, Alfonso VI of León and Castile had occupied Toledo. To bring the Spanish church into line with the Roman, he had given its most important posts to monks of the Benedictine order of Cluny. They, being Frenchmen, were deeply interested in Scholastic philosophy, and so the next archbishop of Toledo, Raymond, set up an institution for translating the work of Arab and Jewish philosophers into Latin. This was done by Spanish Jews, who were often trilingual; and in this way, about the year 1150, a large number of books, including Arab translations of Aristotle, became available to Western Europe. They arrived just when the need for them was greatest, and Avicebrón's *Well of Life* and Averroës's commentaries on Aristotle, to name only two, set off the great movement in Western philosophy that culminated in Albertus Magnus, Thomas Aquinas, and Duns Scotus.

Here again, it was mainly Greek science that the Arabs passed on. Their great physicians, Avicenna and Avenzoar, whose names were household words in the Middle Ages, re-introduced the system of Hippocrates, Dioscorides, and Galen. It was not a very useful system, for it was based on the false theory of the four humors. The skill of their doctors was really founded on clinical experience, little of which found its way into their treatises. In the same way, Arab astronomy was based almost entirely on Ptolemy's *Almagest*, which Gerard of Cremona translated from Arabic into Latin about 1170. But Indian advances in trigonometry, as well as the more exact observations of their own astronomers, had enabled the Arabs to plot the movements of the stars and planets with greater accuracy; for this reason, the Tables of Arzachel of Toledo became the classic work on astronomy for the peoples of northern Europe and so prepared the way for Copernicus and Tycho Brahe.

Thus we see Spanish Islam passing on its acquisitions to other cultures just as it was coming to an end itself. Then in 1610, the Moriscos, as the Moors who had now been forcibly converted to Christianity were called, were expelled from the country. After that, scarcely a trace of Arab or Moorish blood remained in the Iberian Peninsula. Their great gift to the rest of Europe had been the philosophy and science they had passed on, not to the Spaniards, but to the nations of the north. And so, during the darkest age of Western history, the Arabs gave to a little corner of Europe a brilliant civilization.

5

WHEN THE NORMANS INVADED ENGLAND
MORRIS BISHOP

The fateful clash of arms at Hastings was one of the
most decisive and significant battles in history.

The fateful clash of arms at Hastings was one of the most decisive and significant battles in history.

It was a chance encounter that day. The year is uncertain - either 1027 or 1028 - but this much is known: Duke Robert of Normandy, known by some as "The Magnificent" and "The Devil" by others, saw a beautiful young woman by the side of a stream along the road to the castle of Falaise. It is said that she was washing her feet, her skirt tucked high on her legs. He was smitten and swept her away to the castle. Quickly, a son was produced, born in 1028 and known originally as "William the Bastard." His rule and reign would echo through Europe for hundreds of years.

The circumstances of his birth would discolor his character and his life. When he attacked Alençon in 1051, the garrison of an outlying guardhouse hung some hides on their walls and shouted: "Hides for the tanner!" ("Hides" in slang meant "whores.") William burned the thirty-two guardsmen out of their stronghold, cut off their hands and feet, and catapulted their extremities into the city, whose citizens surrendered.

He was a brooding, angry boy. When he was about seven, he was named successor to the dukedom by his father, who then traveled as a pilgrim to Jerusalem and died on the journey. His mother married a viscount and left William in the care of guardians. The nobles immediately disregarded their oaths of fidelity, built forbidden castles, and entered upon a course of mutual extermination. They killed William's guardian and his tutor. A party sought William in his castle bedroom, but stabbed his steward, Osbern, instead, unaware that the boy was clutching him under the tossed bedclothes. He emerged later covered with blood. While his maternal uncle hid him in the homes of nearby peasants and woodcutters, other supporters tracked down the assassins and stabbed them in their beds, according to the precedent they had set.

The savage nobles, and even the king of France, took advantage of the young duke's weakness. But fortunately, they were too jealous of one another to unite effectively against him. William thus was able to assume command of his faithful when barely adolescent. He was familiar with plots, bloodshed, torture, death. He had no boyhood, and evidently no education, except in war. He learned that he must rule or be ruled, kill or be killed. He must fight and win; he must seize and hold. He was taking the character and learning the trade of the Conqueror.

He was tall for his times, at five feet ten inches, and muscular until his later years when he thickened around the middle. He had a harsh, guttural voice. He was devout, temperate in eating and drinking - he hated drunkenness and drinkers - and chaste. He seems never to have had a mistress or concubine. He courted, first for advantage and then for love, Matilda, daughter of the count of Flanders. She was a great match, a descendant of Charlemagne and Alfred the Great of England. She was very small, just a shade over four feet. But she burst with vigor and spirit. The story runs that when the marriage was proposed, she cried: "I would rather be a veiled nun than be given to a bastard!" But William was not a Conqueror for nothing. It is said he invaded her quarters, dragged her around the room by the hair, and kicked her until she gave her consent. Still, the union turned out to be a happy one. Tiny Matilda bore him nine children (possibly ten), gave him constant good advice, and served as regent on occasion.

Across the Channel was England, ruled by Edward ("the Confessor"). His mother was William's great-aunt. He spent most of his life in Normandy until he was summoned to rule England in 1042. Edward was very good, very weak, and childless - more monk than king, everyone said. He packed his government and his church with Normans. William paid him a visit in Westminster and reported afterward that Edward had formally offered him the succession to the English throne. If so, there were no witnesses, and the crown was not his to offer.

The most powerful man in England was Harold, son of Earl Godwin of Wessex and brother of Edward's queen. He was very tall and mighty, Nordic in appearance, and known as an honorable English county gentleman. The England that he controlled, under the king, had a population of about a 1.25 million. It was a civilized land with effective government and administration, laws, currency, communications. It had its own thriving literature and distinctive art and was far more peaceful than Normandy.

Much of what we know - or think we know - about what unfolded next comes from the Bayeux Tapestry, an enormous and extraordinary artifact that is part art, part chronicle, and part history (as with much of history, it is written from the perspective of the winners.) It is believed to have been made in the waning years of the eleventh century, close to the events it portrays. It was rediscovered in the eighteenth century, and since then, its 230 feet of panels and captions have been pored over by historians looking for clues about William's rise to power, both on and off the battlefield.

In 1064, Edward the Confessor was sixty-two and worried about his own future and England's. Out of concern for the first, he was building Westminster Abbey, but his provisions for the second are obscure and disputed. King Edward, then, sent Harold to the Continent, very likely to confirm his choice of William as his successor or to make some sort of deal with him.

Harold undertook the unwelcome task. His ship missed its mark and came ashore near Saint-Valery at the mouth of the Somme, which was the territory of Count Guy de Ponthieu. Count Guy treated him as a shipwrecked sailor clapping him in a dungeon and holding him for a thumping ransom. But Duke

William demanded Harold's release and sent a deputation to conduct him in all honor to Rouen.

William and Harold took an immediate shine to each other. They hunted, hawked, and feasted together, and certainly talked politics. William took Harold to a little war in Brittany and rewarded his prowess by dubbing him a knight. This honor was a trap; according to feudal practice, the knight was bound by fealty to the dubber. William could not bear to let his dear friend depart for England. Finally, he made a bargain: He would give Harold his daughter's hand in marriage and free return to England, but he would require Harold's oath that he would support William's succession to the English throne. Harold agreed, being well aware that an ordinary oath made under duress is not binding.

The ceremony of oath-taking was held in Bayeux, then as now a small provincial city just inland from the Normandy Coast. William had his clergy assemble the holiest relics of the dukedom, and concealed them in a chest. Harold swore to be William's man. And then, as described in the doggerel verse of the Norman chronicler Wace:

Then kneeling, and still with his hand on the Chest

In reverent guise he his lips to it press'd.

As he rose to his feet, the Duke took his hand,

And fast by the Chest bade him still keep his stand;

The Pall he uprais'd, and made Harold aware

How solemn an Oath on such Relics he sware.

And he, when he saw what was hid by the Veil,

And what he had sworn upon, felt his heart quail.

Harold was in a bind. He could not deny having sworn; there were too many witnesses. He could not dismiss the sanctity of the oath; the guarantors were the holy saints themselves. William had got the feudal world, the Church, and heaven itself to support his claim to the English crown.

Harold returned to England to make his ominous report to the king. He dodged marrying William's daughter in ungentlemanly style and ruled England as a sort of prime minister while everyone waited for King Edward to die. In 1065, Harold was forced to depose his troublesome younger brother, Tostig, from his earldom of Northumbria. Tostig went to Flanders and devoted himself to plotting against the English regime.

On January 5, 1066, Edward the Confessor died. On his deathbed, he named Harold heir to the kingdom. Although by English custom, this was actually only a nomination, the nobles quickly met and elected Harold king. On the very day of Edward's burial in the new Westminster Abbey, Harold was crowned by the Archbishop of York.

Thus the terrible year of 1066 began. In April appeared a portent in the heavens - a long-tailed comet, as large as a full moon; it was visible for two weeks. This was Halley's Comet on its seventy-six-year return, said to always bring trouble.

William was now determined to be king of England. He made his preparations with the utmost astuteness. He appealed to public opinion - noble public opinion, of course - by demanding that Harold renounce his usurped crown. He asked the pope's blessing on a punitive expedition into England, a country recalcitrant toward papal authority, lax in enforcing clerical celibacy, and slow to make its required remittances to Rome. The pope replied by authorizing William to invade England and oversee the collection of payments due. He also included a letter of excommunication for Harold and his allies along with a consecrated battle banner. Thus the Western conscience was rallied to support the invader. A dynastic quarrel took on the character of a crusade.

William dealt with his nobles in general councils and in innumerable private interviews. His country was momentarily at peace, and his gentlemen were bored. He made alluring promises of land, loot, rank, and feudal rights in a rich country that had lost the way of war. He went beyond Normandy to tempt adventurers; important contingents from Brittany and Flanders responded. He organized a fifth column of Normans and pro-Normans in England. He entertained Harold's disgruntled brother, Tostig, and encouraged him to make a probing attack on the southern English coast and to form an offensive alliance with the Norwegian king, Harold Hardrada, who had a penchant for lawlessness.

William assembled his men, perhaps 8,000 combatants, plus sailors, grooms, armorers, cooks, and so on. They were quartered along the Norman coast, with headquarters at the mouth of the Dives River, which was then a capacious port northeast of Caen. The knights supplied their own horses, armor, and weapons, but these had to be inspected and supplemented. The chief need was transport; the building of the ships is vividly illustrated in the Bayeux Tapestry. Says Wace:

The Ports of all Normandy teem'd with new life,

Wherever you tuned preparation was rife.

Materials and Timber were haul'd to the shore,

Bolts fashion'd, Planks jointed, or brought out of store:

Boats fitted, Ships rigging, Masts rais'd, Sails outspread,

With foresight and outlay in readiness made.

Military men estimate that the transports numbered about 700. If, as seems likely, they were built to a common plan, this would be a very early example of mass production. The craft resembled the Viking longships, long and narrow with a shallow draft.

Each had a single sail and mast. There were no oars except one for steering; rowers would take too much precious space. The boats could probably not work at all sailing into the wind. William was taking a terrific chance on having a fair following wind and not too much of it. And if his expedition should come to grief, his chances of re-embarkation and return were poor.

It was a brilliant supply operation, which included even a prefabricated fort ready for immediate erection.

The fleet was reported ready in mid-August. Meanwhile, Harold had assembled the English militia, the *fyrd*, to guard against Tostig's raids on the south coast and against the Norman threat. Tostig then went north to plan, with Harold Hardrada, an invasion of England's east coast before winter.

William had now only to wait for a suitable wind to carry him to England. But the breeze blew steadily from the north. During a lull, in mid-September, William moved his fleet northeast along the Norman coast to Saint-Valery-sur-Somme, forty miles nearer England than Dives. Again he sat down to wait in vain for the wind, which had to be exactly right. Or was his delay deliberate? Had his intelligence sources predicted what actually occurred? In early September, Harold was forced to disband his coast-guarding militia, which was eager to harvest the neglected crops. And there is a good likelihood that William was in touch with Tostig and Harold Hardrada and was glad to time his invasion with theirs in the north.

Harold Hardrada, with about 300 Viking dragon ships, entered the Humber, near present-day Leeds, and, by September 18, had pushed upstream to Riccall. His army disembarked and marched on York, nine miles away. The earls of Mercia and Northumberland met him at Gate Fulford. In a long and bloody battle, they were defeated.

When King Harold, in London, got news of the northern invasion, he immediately assembled his permanent troops and available militiamen. His specialties in war were speed and surprise. His army, mounted, went north on the old Roman road, making the 200 miles to York at the rate of forty miles a day, a remarkable feat for both horses and men. He met the Norsemen at Stamford Bridge, beyond York, on September 25. In a great battle, his saddle-sore troops destroyed the enemy and killed Harold Hardrada and Tostig. The invaders, who had come in 300 ships, went home in twenty-four.

Three days after Stamford Bridge, Duke William landed in the south.

On September 27, the persistent west wind at Saint-Valery had shifted to the south. William gave the crucial order. The ships were pulled into the water and loaded with men, horses, and gear. By sunset, the fleet was assembled in the Channel. William took his place in his flagship, seen in the Bayeux Tapestry with its elaborately carved figureheads, fore and aft. He hoisted a masthead beacon, flaming in an iron basket, as a guide. The flotilla reached the coast at Pevensey at 8:30 a.m.

The crossing, although only sixty miles, was a remarkable feat of navigation. The fleet had to find a sandy or shingly beach on which to disembark, and much of the English south coast was cliff or marsh or forbidding shore. Apparently, William aimed for Pevensey and hit it square. The pilots navigated by the stars and intuition, for they had no compasses, and the crescent moon set at 9:15 p.m. Yet only two vessels were lost. One of them carried the expedition's soothsayer. "No great loss," said William; "he couldn't predict his own fate."

Pevensey was a spit of land at the entrance to a shallow tidal harbor, now filled in and transformed into a sheep pasture. A Roman fort stood, and still stands, on the spit. The position is well defensible; a small force of archers could have raised havoc with the Normans wading in from the sea. But the English *fyrd* had gone home, and the landing was unopposed.

The masts were removed, and the boats were hauled in as far as possible. The archers were the first ashore. They fanned out in search of hostile troops and found none. Then the mailed knights and the horses debarked. Finally, the service troops, carpenters, farriers, and cooks descended, unloading supplies and equipment. The efficient amphibious operation was a tribute to the planners. And, like other such operations, it was blessed by the general's good luck.

Disembarking, William stumbled and fell. This was an evil omen. But William cried: "By the splendor of God, I here have taken the land in both my hands!" It is a well-beloved story, although not exactly an original notion. When Julius Caesar landed in Africa, he also fell, then seized the earth, and exclaimed in Latin: *"Teneo te, Africa!"* ("I hold you, Africa!").

William's plan was clear: to seize a strong, defensible beachhead from which he could ravage the countryside, supply his troops, and eventually provoke battle with the enemy under favorable circumstances. For he must fight and conquer quickly. Time was against him. But Pevensey was too narrow and restricted a base. He therefore moved about ten miles east to Hastings, which in those days formed a kind of peninsula protected on three sides by water. (Some historians suggest he may have been aiming for Hastings in the first place.) There he made an entrenched camp and within a day put up his prefabricated fort.

Meanwhile, a faithful Sussex official galloped 250 miles north to inform Harold of the invasion. The news could not have reached him before October 1 or 2. Harold did not waste a moment. He assembled his troops, still battle-sore, and those few archers and militiamen who could be mounted, and rode at top speed to London. It was the second forced march in as many weeks. On the way, he picked up recruits, ordered to follow him on foot. Others joined him in London.

Harold was in a rage. He was provoked by news that William was systematically ravaging and burning the south coast. (The Bayeux Tapestry shows soldiers setting fire to a house while a mother and child escape.) Not waiting for the *fyrd* to assemble from all England, he marched out of London on October 11. He took the highway to Rochester, then turned south on the old Roman way through the dense forest of the Weald to Hastings. His army, mostly dismounted, covered nineteen miles a day. This is amazing speed when one considers the weight of equipment, the ruggedness of the road, the many swamps, thickets, and sharp little hills, and the difficulties of supply in the barely inhabited forest country.

Harold's army, perhaps 9,000 strong, was composed of his own men, known as housecarls, and a contingent of the *fyrd*. According to one review of these troops, the housecarls "were professional men-at-arms who were dressed in short, close-fitting leather jerkins, on which iron rings were sewn, trousers bound with thongs, and sandals. They wore their hair long, and their heads were covered by steel caps with nasal pieces and long leather flaps which fell over their shoulders." They carried pointed shields and Danish battle-axes, with which a horse and rider could be cut down at a blow.

The *fyrd* was composed of peasants, ill-trained if at all. They wore leather jerkins and caps and were armed with farm tools, such as scythes and pitchforks, and miscellaneous spears, short axes, and slings. Very few were archers. But at least they had Saxon courage and the Englishman's hatred of the invader.

On the evening of October 13, Harold emerged from the forest and encamped on the edge of open farmland, recently harvested. His position was on Caldbec Hill, in the present village of Battle, seven miles from Hastings shore and perhaps three or four from William's camp.

William's scouts promptly informed him of Harold's arrival. He had an immediate choice to make. He could await Harold's move against his entrenched camp, or he could attack. If he waited, Harold might also wait, until overwhelming reinforcements should arrive. He chose to attack while the English were still disorganized. He moved north at dawn on the fourteenth. He found the English deploying in a very strong position just below the summit of a small hill, with their flanks protected by marshy streams and with open fields before them.

Halfway down the slope, William deployed his army, with the archers foremost, the cavalry next, the infantry in the rear. The banner blessed by the pope waved overhead. William, wearing a bag of relics at his throat, rode back and forth giving final orders.

His minstrel Taillefer, the eternal exhibitionist, gained William's permission to strike the first blow. He rode in front of the Normans chanting a song about Roland, the legendary hero, tossed his sword high in the air, and caught it by the hilt. He then galloped straight at the enemy, and with spear under arm impaled an Englishman. His victory was short lived. He was quickly chopped down by battle axes.

Now the Norman archers moved forward to their effective range of about 100 yards and let loose a volley. But they were shooting uphill against men crouching behind their shields. The chief product of the attack was a chorus of gibes and taunts. The archers' arrows were soon exhausted. They depended for replenishment on picking up the opponents' spent shafts, and there were few to collect.

The next stage is not clear. Perhaps a cavalry charge followed as always by an infantry assault.

The attackers had the advantage of armor, being mostly clad in linked chain mail, and they were probably more agile than the English in thrusting with their long swords. But they were fighting uphill; and the English had the advantage of reach with their five-foot axes, which could sever a horse's neck or cleave a helmet or a mailed shoulder, driving the chain-mail links into the wound.

The battle resolved itself, then, into a series of hand-to-hand engagements. At length, the Breton contingent on William's left wavered and fell back. The English broke ranks and started in pursuit. The rumor ran among the Normans that William was killed. He doffed his helmet and rode to and fro reassuring his men, sending his mounted knights to ride down and pick off the scattered English one by one.

A long lull followed while both armies reformed. William launched his cavalry in full force against the English position. They were met by a storm of stones, javelins, and Saxon throwing axes. The fighting was long, fierce, and bloody. Harold's two brothers were killed, but the English line held.

According to the Norman chroniclers, William now practiced one of the oldest tricks in the military bag, the "Feigned Retreat." But this trick is also one of the most difficult; it requires perfect battlefield control and timing and well-trained troops, or else the feigned retreat is very likely to turn into a real one. Modern military men are inclined to think that the Norman cavalry in the center gave way, and that the English broke ranks to pursue them. The temptation would have been great; the field was covered with dead and wounded Norman knights. Each wore an expensive suit of chain mail, the most precious of loot. The Bayeux Tapestry shows many scenes of survivors pulling coats of mail over the heads of dead men, in some cases apparently first removing the head.

William seized his opportunity. He ordered his cavalry on left and right to close in on the pursuers. In the open, the horsemen were easily able to run down and destroy the foot soldiers.

William now ordered a direct attack in full strength on the English position. The Normans, massed and fierce for victory, broke through the English defense. One chronicler said that the dead stood so close they had hardly room to fall. Panicking Englishmen began to run for the shelter of the forest. Harold was struck down by Norman knights. On the spot where his rival fell, William decreed that the altar of a great commemorative church, Battle Abbey, should stand.

The Normans had won the battle and the war. Harold and all his brothers were dead; there was no other serious claimant, besides William, for the English crown. During the remainder of the campaign, William moved cautiously, consolidating his hold on the southeast. He circled about London, entered the city, and on Christmas Day, 1066, was crowned king of the English in Westminster Abbey.

The day of Hastings, October 14, 1066, was one of the decisive days of all history. The battle itself was nip and tuck; the shift of a few elements and a bit of luck could have given the victory to the Anglo-Saxons.

If Harold had won at Hastings and had survived, William would have had no choice but to renounce his adventure. He could not have prevailed against the aroused masses of the island, led by their determined king. He could not possibly have raised reinforcements in France. There is little likelihood that anyone would have attempted an invasion of England during the next millennium. England would have strengthened its bonds with Scandinavia while remaining distrustful of the western Continent. The native Anglo-Saxon culture, art, and literature would have developed in unimaginable ways. The English language would not exist; it would be Anglo-Saxon. And William the Conqueror would be dimly known in history only as William the Bastard.

6

THE BYZANTINES
ALFRED DUGGAN

The achievement of the Byzantines (who called themselves
"Romans") was to keep barbarians at bay, create a new art,
preserve Western culture for 1,000 years, and push a little
further the limits of both piety and depravity.

The achievement of the Byzantines (who called themselves "Romans") was to keep barbarians at bay, create a new art, preserve Western culture for 1,000 years, and push a little further the limits of both piety and depravity.

It is only recently that the word "Byzantium" has been freed from the contempt attached to it by generations of uncomprehending, humanist-minded historians. Preeminent among them was Edward Gibbon, for whom Byzantine history was "a tedious and uniform tale of weakness and misery" in which "not a single discovery was made to exalt the dignity or promote the happiness of mankind." Christian Byzantium - or rather the triumph of Christianity itself - marked for Gibbon the end of the "classical" civilization he so much admired, marked indeed the decline and fall of the Roman Empire. At the end of his vast work, *The History of the Decline and Fall of the Roman Empire*, published between 1776 and 1788, he notes: "I have described the triumph of barbarism and religion."

Some 100 years later, historian William Lecky was still echoing Gibbon's dismissive view: "Of that Byzantine Empire, the universal verdict of history is that it constitutes, without a single exception, the most thoroughly base and despicable form that civilization has yet assumed . . . [It] is a monotonous story of the intrigues of priests, eunuchs, and women, of poisonings, of conspiracies, of uniform ingratitude, of perpetual fratricides."

Judgments like this are not likely to be made to-day. Byzantine history and civilization have become legitimate objects of academic attention. Byzantine society is no longer regarded as the stagnant playground of decadent voluptuaries, immersed in sensuality and bestirring themselves only when provoked by some outburst of public spleen in the Hippodrome, or by some hair-splitting theological subtlety thrown into their midst by fanatic monks. In art, literature, statesmanship, diplomacy, and war, Byzantium's achievements are now recognized, even admired. The philosopher Alfred North Whitehead went so far as to assert that its culture was superior to that of classical Rome. Some historians have claimed that it afforded greater opportunities for living a civilized life than the Pax Augusta. It might, in fact, seem that the wheel has come full circle, and that Gibbon's thesis is being reversed: It is no longer a question of Rome's decline and fall, but of Byzantium's ascent and triumph.

The Byzantine Empire was not simply the Roman Empire extended through another 1,000-odd years of slow ossification and decay.

This was a new creation, growing out of the Roman past but essentially different from it. Indeed, it was precisely a failure of ideology in the Empire of the Caesars that made a new form of society imperative if Western civilization was to survive. Already in the second century CE, the Roman Empire was threatened with disruption. There were civil wars within and frontier wars without; legions mutinied, Goths and Parthians bestirred themselves. The highly centralized administrative machinery creaked under the strain. Disaster was averted for the time being by Diocletian, who came to power in 284. He introduced a series of measures to decentralize and stabilize the Empire, now split for this purpose into four great compartments. But these reforms only postponed matters. After his death, struggles broke out among the rulers of the various parts of the Empire as they contended for the imperial throne. And it was only in 323 that the triumphant survivor was able to take the steps that created the empire of the Byzantines.

This survivor was Constantine the Great. He was born in CE 272 in Moesia, in present-day Serbia, and as a youth was sent to the court of Nicomedia in Asia Minor, which Diocletian had already chosen for his headquarters in preference to Rome. After serving in Persia and Egypt, he was acclaimed Caesar at York, in England, where his father, a political and military advisor and Senior Western Emperor, had died while on an expedition against the Scots. The next six years Constantine spent in Gaul and Italy as co-emperor with Maxentius, and in 312, he captured Rome from his colleague. This made him sole emperor in the West, with Licinius, sole emperor in the East, his only rival. His final triumph did not come until 323 with the defeat and capture of Licinius.

Faced now with the task of arresting the disintegration of the Empire and of welding its heterogeneous elements, both territorial and cultural, into a new coherence, Constantine made it his first concern to choose and construct a new imperial capital. Where should this be? Rome was the scene of conspiracy and intrigue, while to the north and west were lands of barbarity. The East seemed the obvious choice because it was the main focus of trade, the place to resist the Parthians and check the westerly migrations from the steppes, and it was where Christianity was rapidly gaining followers. And if the East was obvious, what better site could there be than the small town of Byzantium? Set on a triangular peninsula commanding the mouth of the Bosporus, which links the Sea of Marmara with the Black Sea and divides Europe from Asia, Byzantium seemed to meet all the requirements. The climate was cool and healthy. Along one side of the triangular peninsula was an inlet known as the Golden Horn that formed a perfect natural harbor. To the south lay the Aegean and the rich gardens of Asia Minor, source of all the earth's fruits, and beyond, the flax fields of Egypt. To the east, as far as India and China, stretched the trade routes along which passed spices and ivory and porcelain and other riches, the raw materials of Byzantine cuisine and art. To the north lay Russia and the Black Sea ports through which flowed wheat and furs, honey and gold, wax and slaves. Byzantium was easily defended, as Constantine had discovered during the war with Licinius, and he must have sensed possibilities as he chose this site and marked out its boundaries. For more than 1,000 years, it was to be the focus of Western civilization.

Edifice after imperial edifice began to rise on the spacious platform, once the ancient acropolis, of the peninsula that divided the Sea of Marmara from the still waters of the Golden Horn. To the east of this platform was the Senate House; to the south was the Great Palace, a dense group of buildings stretching through gardens down to the shore; to the west lay the Forum and the vast theatre of the Hippodrome, capable of seating 40,000 people and containing works of art Constantine had rifled from the entire classical world. Northeast of the Hippodrome, on the headland most visible to ships approaching from the south, Constantine placed the Church of the Holy Wisdom, Hagia Sophia. Enlarged by his son Constantius and rebuilt in the sixth century by the emperor Justinian, it was eventually to be recognized as the crowning glory of the Empire.

Constantine also set up a huge column rising from a white marble plinth and supporting a Greek Apollo whose head was replaced by that of the Emperor encircled with the golden rays of the sun. Within the plinth were enshrined such purported relics of special veneration as a casket holding crumbs from the bread with which Christ fed the 5,000, the adze with which Noah built the ark, the alabaster box of ointment with which Mary anointed Jesus, and the crosses of the two thieves crucified with Jesus of Nazareth which the Emperor's mother, Saint Helena of York, had recently brought from Jerusalem. The inscription on the plinth of Constantine's column read: "0 Christ, Ruler and Master of the World, to Thee have I now consecrated this obedient City." In May of CE 330, the city was solemnly dedicated and the Byzantine Empire inaugurated.

For this empire, Constantine the Great laid both the temporal and spiritual foundations and fused together the political legacy of Rome, the cultural legacy of the Hellenic world, and the explosive dynamism of the Christian faith. It was to last for 1,123 years and to be governed by no less than eighty-eight rulers in succession.

For convenience, this long period can be divided into phases. The first - from the founding of Constantinople in 330 to the death of the emperor Anastasius in 518 - was one of growth and trial. Thanks partly to its geographical position, the city escaped the barbarian devastations that visited the West. Only in one battle, at Adrianople in 378, were the armies of the Eastern Empire defeated by the Goths.

The second phase, from 518 to 610, or from Justin I to Phocas, is marked above all by the reign, from 527-565, of the emperor Justinian and his wife, Theodora. Fired by an ambition to bring within the orbit of Byzantium all those alienated lands of the old Roman Empire and to establish his government over the whole of the Mediterranean and Western world, Justinian embarked on a policy of expansion that strained the resources of the empire to their limits. From 533-554, he brought northern Africa, Italy, southern Spain, and the islands of Sicily, Corsica, Sardinia, and the Balearics under Byzantine rule. He also initiated a series of internal reforms to quell civil unrest. In spite of the wealth and splendor of the imperial capital, the whole administrative machinery was in urgent need of overhaul. So great was popular discontent over the various abuses that in 532, a revolt known as the Nika riot broke out at Constantinople and nearly cost the ruler his throne. That it did not was due to the courage of Theodora and to the loyalty and brutality of the imperial guards who, after half the original city of Constantinople had been burned to the ground, put down the revolt by slaughtering some 30,000 of the insurgents in the Hippodrome.

Justinian, in order to remove the causes of the riot, set about at once to centralize the administration, abolishing the sale of offices and tightening up provincial government. But his greatest work, already begun in the opening years of his reign, was the recodification of Roman law. In a series of volumes, collectively known as the Codex Justinianus, the primary rules of social existence as defined by Roman law were reformulated in accordance with the Christian ethic. It became the civil code not only of Byzantium but of much of the Western world in subsequent centuries. Finally, Justinian set about repairing the damage caused to the capital by riot.

Various new civic buildings were erected, and a bronze equestrian statue of the Emperor himself, wearing what was referred to as the armor of Achilles, was set up on a huge column in the main public square, the Augustaeum. Above all, the great church of Constantinople, Hagia Sophia, had to be reconstructed. In five years and ten months, the two major architects, Isidore the Milesian and Anthemius of Tralles, raised a building that was from then on the pride and pivot of the Byzantine world, a visible expression of the vital consciousness - forged from Roman, Greek, and Christian elements - of the Byzantine people.

That amalgamation notwithstanding, Byzantium was above all a Christian empire; before we can understand its unique nature, we must try to discern what meaning and relevance this fact had for the Byzantincs themselves. Here we may have recourse to the image of the dome. Set over all, seeming to contain and embrace in its simple unity all the diversity and multitude that lies below it, the dome is the Byzantine architectural form par excellence. And the dome of all Byzantine domes was that of Hagia Sophia. It was a dome so light, as the contemporary historian Procopius wrote, that it "does not appear to rest upon a solid foundation, but to cover the place beneath as though it were suspended from heaven by the fabled golden chain."

This description is not merely figurative. In the sixth century, Paul the Silentiary called the dome a "great helmet, which bending over like the radiant heavens embraces the church." The language is one of an intelligible symbolism. It was this desire to make visible a certain complex of ideas that impelled the emperor Justinian and the subsequent builders of Byzantine architecture to give such prominence to the dome and to the building of domed churches and palaces. It was natural that the visitor who approached the holy city of Constantinople from across the Sea of Marmara, and rounded the promontory to enter the Golden Horn saw rising on the spacious platform of the headland the huge domed mass of Hagia Sophia.

For this church expressed that consciousness of a transcendent reality, of a supernatural presence, that lay at the heart of Byzantine life. It was a replica of heaven upon earth, of Paradise, of the house of God. And the crowning glory of the church was the dome, invested with a symbolism both divine and royal. This half-divine, half-royal symbolism was transferred to the dome of the Christian church and was there linked with the majesty of Christ. It was his image, as Christ Pantocrator, the Almighty, that animated the space of the dome. The dome symbolized transcendent power and authority as well as the Resurrection and the coming of the Kingdom of God in which human life and society would be fulfilled. In it were thus embodied the multiple ideals and purposes which gave Byzantium its raison d'être and which the Empire, in theory at least, was consciously intended to realize.

But if Christ was the spiritual ruler of Byzantium, his temporal instrument for achieving the corporate salvation of his chosen nation was the Christian emperor. Although formally elected by the Senate and proclaimed by the people and the army, the emperor was in fact regarded as chosen by divine decree and therefore as occupying a position superior to that of other mortals. "Glory to God who has designated you as basileus, who has glorified you, who has manifested His grace to you" ran the acclamation which followed the imperial coronation. Temporal representative of Christ, the emperor was equal to the Apostles. His costume was like an icon. At Easter he donned the garb of resurrection, and appeared surrounded by twelve apostles, his body swathed in white bands. Twelve guests sat at his table at meals. His receptions were not so much audiences as epiphanies, divine appearances. They took place in the Sacred Palace in an octagonal room crowned with an immense cupola and furnished with glittering chandeliers, golden lions, golden griffins, golden birds perched on golden branches. At the heart of all this, on the imperial throne, was the sovereign himself, clothed in gold, bathed in sanctity. What he touched was sacred. To insult him was to blaspheme. To revolt against his authority was to invite excommunication. Rebellion was apostasy. And this sanctity of the sovereign flowed over into that of his ministers and the whole imperial administration.

Indeed, this civil service - massive and proficient -

was the backbone of the state. Down to Justinian's day it used Latin as its official language. But from the seventh century onward, the service gradually assumed a new form. Greek became the official language. Greek designations replaced the Latin titles of ministers and high officials. Of these, the most numerous were the *logothetes*, ministers of internal and foreign affairs, of public revenues and imperial estates, and of the military chest. Generally, these great functionaries were required to pass an entrance exam and were recruited from distinguished families with a tradition of public service. They were nominated, promoted, and dismissed by the emperor, and the power remained with him.

If the regulation and administration of the material and temporal side of life lay with the emperor and his service, the spiritual and eternal side of life was most fully represented by the monasteries and hermitages, rather than the bishops and clergy as might be expected. It is impossible to overestimate the significance of the role played by monasticism in Byzantium. It was not simply that monasteries were places in which deposed emperor and downtrodden peasant alike could find refuge - a kind of safety valve through which rejected or disruptive elements might be discharged without the system exploding. It was that the monasteries were the forges of what the Byzantines regarded as the highest types of humanity in which the Christian ideal was realized to the fullest possible extent on earth. The emperor might be God's elect. The saint or the holy man was more: He was a living bundle of divine energies, the incarnation of the Holy Spirit, witness of God, and in a certain sense, God himself. For the Byzantines saw the highest type of humanity fulfilled not in those who lived a good life, but in those who through earnest battle had broken the barrier between man and God and had fused the two once more.

The saint or the holy man was a mediator between earth and heaven. He was a present source of mercy, miracle, and guidance, the father of the people among whom he dwelt, their healer and deliverer. They were fanatics, but from their ranks came the men and women who guarded the empire's conscience, its spiritual lifeblood, and achievements.

Between the material and the temporal, represented in Byzantium by the emperor and the body politic, and the spiritual and the eternal, represented by the saints, there was the image-forming world of the soul and of the imagination. This was the world of Byzantine art, which not only gave expression to the divine and supernatural aspirations of humankind, but also to those transcendental realities which are the objects of his spiritual quest.

The first flowering of Byzantine art began with the founding of Constantinople and reached its golden age under Justinian in the sixth century. This period coincided with the final decadence of Hellenistic art, which had spread across the Mediterranean and

Anatolian world from Rome to central Asia. It was unrooted and cosmopolitan, dominated by the natural world and with the natural human form as its final measure and norm. Byzantine art may be seen as the result of the imposition of Oriental forms on a Hellenistic ground. At the same time there came about the architectural fusion of the early Christian basilica (square atrium or narthex, rounded apse, and long naves flanked by twin or quadruple rows of pillars) with the domed octagon or rotunda - a fusion crystallized in Justinian's new church of Hagia Sophia. "Solomon, I have surpassed thee," Justinian is reported to have said when first he viewed the immense majesty of the completed edifice.

Justinian's attempt to reconstitute the Roman Empire proved politically a great burden, and the next phase of Byzantine history, opening with the reign of Heraclius in 610 and ending with that of Theodosius III in 717, was one in which the existence of the whole empire was imperiled. First came the onslaughts of the Persian armies under Khosrau II in the East, followed by the attacks of the Avars and the Lombards in the West. Then, in 634, within three years after the death of Muhammad, his followers from Medina attacked the Byzantine garrisons of Palestine. By 640, Palestine was lost and Egypt invaded. Heraclius died the next year, Alexandria was evacuated, and Persia and Armenia were overrun. Cyprus fell, and in 655, the Byzantine fleet, under Emperor Constans II, was defeated off the coast of Lycia, in what is now southern Turkey. But largely as a result of the discovery and effective use of a new weapon, so-called Greek fire, the Muslims were finally brought to a halt on both land and sea, and in 678, peace was concluded. Greatly reduced in size, the Byzantine Empire was from then on centered on Constantinople and the Greek seaboard, while connections with the West grew correspondingly weaker; for instance, the last vestiges of Latin were dropped from official imperial usage.

The fourth phase, from 717 to 867, began with a restoration of the prestige of Byzantine arms under the Isaurian emperors Leo and Constantine V Copronymus. During the start of this era, the Muslims attacked again and laid siege to Constantinople itself, but they were defeated by the Byzantine forces, combined with frost and famine which were said to have brought death to 150,000 troops. That defeat stemmed for a time the tide of Arab expansion.

But the great event of this phase of Byzantine history lay not in the field of military triumph or internal reform, but in religion. The worship of sacred images, or icons, had by this time become an integral part of Orthodox Christianity. And thus when Emperor Leo, supported by his puritanical followers from the hinterland of Asia Minor, launched an attack on image worship in an edict of 726, reaction was immediate and intense. Riots in the capital were soon followed by insurrection in Greece. Byzantine authority in Italy was fatally undermined, and the whole Empire was split asunder. Even the restoration of the worship of images by the empress Irene in 787 did not bring an end to the troubles. Then in 813, with the advent of a new emperor from Armenia, icons were once again proscribed. It was only because most orthodox Christians, and particularly the monks, remained so intransigent in their attachment to sacred pictures that the iconoclasts, or "image-breakers," were finally defeated.

The restoration of images after these struggles ushered in a new period of Byzantine art, which continued through the eleventh and twelfth centuries.

A single dynasty, the Macedonians, filled the 200 years between 867 and 1057. It was a period of territorial expansion and internal prosperity, in which Islamic advances were repelled and many of the lost provinces and cities of the East were reclaimed. In 961, the capture of Crete restored control of the Aegean to the Byzantine navy, and by 1014, Emperor Basil II Bulgaroctonos (the Bulgar-slayer) had reduced the whole Balkan Peninsula to imperial rule. External success was marked by a corresponding prodigality at home. All the world's wealth seemed to pour through the trade routes of the Levant, overland from India and beyond, or down the great Russian rivers and the Black Sea into Constantinople, there to furnish fresh magnificence in art and architecture. The only signs of trouble to come were the increasing independence of the great feudal overlords, the growing alienation of the West, soon to lead to an official schism with Rome, and the deepening shadow of the Seljuk Turks converging on the northeast frontiers.

With the death of the last ruler of the Macedonian house in 1053, a thirty-year struggle for the possession of the throne broke out among the great feudal families, only resolved by the accession, in 1081, of Alexius I Comnenus, succeeded in turn by his son and grandson. Meanwhile, the Seljuk Turks were continuing to expand, and in 1071, they routed the Byzantine armies in eastern Anatolia, taking the emperor Romanus IV Diogenes prisoner. This was the prelude to the loss of the greater part of Byzantine territory in Asia Minor. Six years later, the Turks occupied Jerusalem, inciting the chivalry of the West. The First Crusade was launched by the Council of Clermont in 1095. Already relationships between the Orthodox Christian churches and the church at Rome had been strained beyond the breaking point, and a state of open schism had been proclaimed and ratified by Patriarch and Pope alike. The result was that the crusaders considered the residents of Byzantium neither Christians nor brothers, as legitimate a target as the Muslims themselves. The Second Crusade in 1147, led by the emperor Conrad Hohenstaufen and King Louis VII of France, looted and raped its way through Byzantine lands till its final defeat by the Turks. As part of the Third Crusade of 1189, a Norman-Sicilian fleet sacked the Greek city of Salonika with particular brutality. But it was with the Fourth Crusade that the full depredation of the West broke over the Byzantines. In 1204, the Latins took Constantinople; the city was handed over to plunder, and its accumulated treasures, including those works of classical art which Constantine the Great had brought to his capital, were destroyed. It is one of the cruel ironies of history that it was the soldiers of the Cross who were responsible for the rape of the queen of Christian cities, preparing the way for the overthrow of the Christian empire.

During the Latin occupation of Constantinople, the Byzantine capital was transferred to Nicaea in Asia Minor. What followed was a series of ham-fisted leadership and petty squabbling, while the Byzantines in exile waited for their chance. It came in 1261, when Michael VIII Palaeologus used a treaty with the Republic of Genoa to bring his forces from Nicaea to Constantinople, recapturing the heart and soul of Byzantium.

And so the Byzantine Empire, diminished but still vigorous, entered upon the final phase of its history, under the dynasty of the Palaeologi. The period was one of rear-guard actions against overwhelming odds. The Empire itself was confined to Nicaea and the northwest corner of Asia Minor, Constantinople and Thrace, Salonika and part of Macedonia, and a few islands. The capital had been devastated and deserted, and its enemies and rivals encroached from all directions. After the death of Michael VIII in 1282, civil war broke out. Meanwhile, the Turks were gradually advancing. By 1345, they had crossed from Asia Minor to Europe. Soon they had overrun the whole Balkan Peninsula, and it was only their defeat by the army of the Mongol ruler Timur in 1402 that prevented them from taking Constantinople itself. Even so, the respite was short. Some twenty years later, the Turks had entered Albania and the Peloponnesus. Salonika was captured in 1430. In a last desperate attempt to secure help from the West, Emperor John VIII Palaeologus tried to persuade his bishops to cede to the demands of the Roman Church. Union between the Orthodox and Latin churches was actually celebrated at Florence in 1439. But it proved an empty formality: the monks in Constantinople didn't accept the accord and the help that Rome sent was insufficient. The Byzantines held out as long as they could, but the end was coming, accelerated by Mehmed the Conqueror becoming the leader of the Ottoman Turks in 1451.

Mehmed II brought his giant artillery into action, and the final preparations for assault were made. Within the city, the last Byzantine emperor, Constantine XI Dragases Palaeologus, remained with his people despite frequent appeals to escape. On the afternoon of May 28, 1453, the last Christian service was held in the great church of Hagia Sophia. Relics and icons were brought out. After the service, Emperor and Patriarch bade public farewell. Then all took their posts to await the attack. It came the next morning before the sun rose. A breach was forced in the great walls, and the Sultan's soldiers poured through. The Emperor, discarding the insignia of his office, plunged into the fighting and was killed on the ramparts. Constantinople fell, and with its fall, the Byzantine Empire was at an end.

The old theory was that the fall of Constantinople was the spark for the Renaissance by setting loose a flood of scholars and classical manuscripts upon the Italian world. That's been discarded. What remains is the understanding that the Byzantine world was the bridge between the ancient Greco-Roman world and the Renaissance, modernity itself. It was a living heritage of art and literature, nurtured and protected and then ready to be rediscovered when the modern world was ready for it.

7

RICHARD AND SALADIN
ALFRED DUGGAN

When they met in bloody war for the Holy Land, the
champions of Christendom and Islam gave the
medieval world a lesson in the honor of kings.

When they met in bloody war for the Holy Land, the champions of Christendom and Islam gave the medieval world a lesson in the honor of kings.

On June 8, 1191, King Richard Coeur de Lion joined the besiegers of the then-Palestinian port city of Acre, who in a curious turn of events were themselves besieged by the great army of Saladin. Richard was thirty-three and already a veteran, leading armies since he was sixteen. He was not only a brave knight but also a skilled commander, especially expert in siege craft and in the dull business of looking after supplies. He was tall and fair and handsome and was as well known for his poetry as for his courage. He loved beauty in every form and could inspire in his followers a lifelong devotion. But there were weaknesses in his character. His witty poet's tongue could turn sharp and acidic; in any company, he must be first; he was stern, unyielding, combative and greedy.

For two years, he had been England's king, but his throne was not secure; John, his younger brother, would displace him if he could. Nonetheless, he and King Philip of France had sworn to reclaim the Holy Land together. After a winter in Sicily and a detour by Richard to Cyprus, they moved on separately to join the Third Crusade already in progress on the Palestine coast.

On the European continent, France and England had been quarreling for a generation. Recently, Richard had made matters worse by refusing to marry Philip's sister Alice, to whom he had been betrothed since childhood, giving as reason the rumors that she had been his father's mistress. To clinch the matter, Richard's mother brought Princess Berengaria of Navarre down to Sicily, and Richard married her on the island of Cyprus.

Relations between the two monarchs could scarcely have been worse. And although Richard had brought to Acre a finer body of troops and a larger sum of money than Philip, he could not command an army that contained the king of France because, as duke of Aquitaine, he had previously done homage to Philip. So Richard's intention was to clear up the mess in Palestine and get home as soon as possible before trouble broke out in England.

However, the mess in this part of the world, known as *Outremer* (French for "overseas") presented many complications. Almost 100 years earlier, in 1095, Pope Urban II had called upon Christian Europe to rescue the Holy Land from the infidels. In that First Crusade, groups of Frankish and Norman knights had assembled large retinues, crossed Europe, fought their way through Asia Minor, and finally managed to wrest Jerusalem from its Egyptian rulers.

But these restless, ambitious adventurers had come to make their own fortunes as much as to restore the Holy Places. Each knight seized and secured what he could for himself, warring constantly with his Christian neighbors. Thus, the Christian community was scarcely unified. It consisted principally of the kingdom of Jerusalem, which stretched from the Egyptian border to Beirut, and three associated states of Antioch, Edessa, and Tripoli, covering what is now Syria, southeast Turkey, and Lebanon. Edessa was retaken by the Muslims in 1144; its fall occasioned a second and wholly unsuccessful crusade.

Each of the remaining states was governed by hereditary descendants of the original knights, who carried on the feuds of their forebears. Toward the end of the twelfth century, the king of Jerusalem, a leper, died childless, leaving two sisters whose marriages assumed supreme political importance. Sibylla, the elder sister, married Guy de Lusignan, a native of France, and they became king and queen of Jerusalem. Her teenage half-sister, Isabella, married Humphrey of Toron (now southern Lebanon), the son of a native baron.

King Guy was heartily disliked by the local lords because he was both ineffectual and a foreigner. The ensuing quarrels so weakened the Christian community that in 1187, Saladin, sultan of Egypt and Syria, marched upon the Christians at Hattin, near present-day Tiberias, captured King Guy, and destroyed most of the Christian forces. The Muslims then swept through Judea, taking the Holy City and many castles of the hill country. When news of this disaster reached Europe, the pope called for a third crusade.

By the end of the year, the Christians held only the seaport of Tyre, and that city had been preserved by a strange stroke of luck. Its frightened defenders had already asked for terms when Conrad of Montferrat (now northwest Italy), arriving from Constantinople, rallied the city to hold out until reinforcements could save it. Conrad became, thereby, a local hero. Most of the lay barons throughout Outremer rallied to him, and it was suggested that he marry Princess Isabella, which would at least give him a rival claim to the throne of Guy and Sibylla.

Conrad was said to have left one wife in Italy and another in Constantinople, and Isabella's marriage to Humphrey of Toron was annulled against her will. She liked the gentle, charming young man who had been kind to her, and she did not at all fancy the rough old soldier. (It is said that Humphrey, who had homosexual leanings, had neglected to consummate the marriage. Later, he and Richard, who also was rumored to be fond of handsome young men, became close friends, which did not help matters.)

When King Philip of France reached Acre in April 1191, six weeks before Richard, he encountered a strong movement to displace King Guy and make Conrad king of Jerusalem. The barons of the kingdom, sprung from French families, treated Philip as their natural lord; he, in turn, willingly supported their favorite, Conrad. Richard, upon arrival, backed Guy, partly because he refused to accept any of Philip's notions and partly because King Guy came from

Richard's French domain of Poitou. Shortly thereafter, a compromise was made whereby Guy would retain the crown during his lifetime (Sibylla had died without surviving issue), and then Conrad would assume the throne. This decision pleased no one and lasted only eight months.

Richard had other enemies. Because his sister Matilda was married to Henry the Lion, a hated foe of the Hohenstaufen emperors, the German Crusaders who preceded both the French and the English at Acre also distrusted him. Thus, Richard went into battle with the French, most of the native barons, and the Germans - all hostile to him for different reasons.

But Saladin, encamped behind the besiegers of Acre, saw only that the Christian army had been reinforced by a mighty warrior. He made even greater efforts to relieve his blockaded city, for a great defeat might destroy his power.

Saladin was a self-made sultan. He lacked the prestige of hereditary rule, and unless he led his men to victory and plunder, they would desert him. His horsemen were Kurds (he was himself a Kurd) or Turks; his foot soldiers, Sudanese; and his indispensable sappers and miners, Egyptian. All his soldiers hated the climate of the unhealthy coast, ravaged and stinking after four years of war. They would not stay unless they were paid punctually, and the money to pay them could come only from Egypt.

In 1191, Saladin was fifty-three and in poor health. But the Holy War was the great objective of his life.

Saladin had won his dominions in war, but he did not charge at the head of his troops. In battle, his station was with the reserve; there is no record that he ever used his sword, save to kill unarmed prisoners after victory. Yet he was fearless, and if his army seemed to be beaten, he would hold his ground to the last.

In every respect, he was the pattern of a Muslim ruler. Though he never found time to make the pilgrimage to Mecca, he said his prayers regularly and kept the fast of Ramadan. He loved to listen to readings from the holy books, even while he rode down the front of a hostile army.

He was a charitable man, also known for being just and for keeping his word, even to Christians. When Jerusalem surrendered to him, 60,000 Christian refugees were in the town, and he set their ransom at the moderate figure of ten dinars per person. The money in the city treasury was applied toward this ransom, though Saladin might have claimed it as booty; to please his brother Saphadin, he freed 1,000 captives and permitted the patriarch to beg off another 700.

As a young man, he had fought in the Egyptian civil wars alongside the army of Christian Jerusalem; it was said that he had been knighted by old Humphrey of Toron, grandfather of young Humphrey.

He knew the type of behavior expected from Christian knights, and though he was not habitually chivalrous, he could answer chivalry in kind. When in 1183 he suddenly attacked Kerak, that remote castle southeast of the Dead Sea was full of guests attending the wedding of Humphrey of Toron and Princess Isabella. With cheerful defiance, the châtelaine (lady of the castle) announced that since the great sultan had come to the wedding, he must share in the feast, and she sent out her servants with the best dishes and the best wine. In return, Saladin gave orders that the tower that sheltered bride and bridegroom must not be bombarded.

We know nothing of Saladin's married life, but he had seventeen sons and at least one daughter and took pains to bring them up properly. Once, he forbid his sons to join in a massacre of Christian prisoners, explaining to his puzzled councilors that the children were too young to understand the true religion. If they were encouraged to kill helpless Christians, he reasoned, they might think it right to kill helpless Muslims.

When Richard reached the camp before Acre in June 1191, the Muslim and Christian armies had been in close contact for three years and truces – both official and unofficial - were frequent. It was natural that Richard, as soon as he arrived, should send envoys to Saladin; he was eager to meet the champion of Islam, who in a single battle had overthrown a kingdom. His first request was merely for an interview.

Saladin answered that kings should not meet while they were at war, though if peace came, he would be delighted to see him. Though Richard tried this approach on several occasions, the two leaders never met except on the battlefield.

Richard was curious to learn more about his great antagonist. Again, he sent his envoy, a Moroccan noble who had long been a captive in Christian hands. This time, his mission was frivolous. The envoy announced that Richard had some fine hawks he would like to send as a present to Saladin, but the hawks were sick, and in the besieged camp, they could not get the fresh food they needed. Would Saladin please send them some chickens?

Saladin willingly sent the poultry, though he said with a laugh that he knew Richard would eat them. He added a suggestion that any further envoys be sent to Saphadin, his brother and the second lord in his dominions. Saladin may have been genuinely busy, or this may have been a barbed reminder that, while King Philip lay before Acre, Richard was only the second lord in the Christian army.

Throughout July, envoys passed to and fro. Richard sent the hawks and other Western curiosities; Saladin, in return, sent fruit, a precious luxury in the blockaded camp. There was a sound political reason for these contacts. The Muslim leaders in Acre were preparing to surrender, and Richard wished to make sure that Saladin knew it.

The surrender took place on July 12. In the tangled negotiations that followed, Richard spoke for the whole Christian army. The Muslims in Acre had offered to buy their lives by handing over three things that were not theirs to give: a large sum of money, the True Cross (captured at Hattin), and 100 named Christian knights. Saladin eagerly collected the money; he was reluctant to hand over the True Cross, though he would probably have done so under pressure; but he failed to produce the named prisoners. On August 11, Richard's envoys refused to accept the money alone. On August 20, recognizing that the agreed ransom would never be handed over, Richard killed the soldiers in the surrendered garrison, along with their wives and children, some 2,700 people in all, excluding some wealthy emirs who bought their survival through the payment of individual ransoms.

Having gained one impressive victory, Richard decided to march sixty miles south to Jaffa, part of present-day Tel Aviv, which had fallen to the Muslims after Hattin. On September 5, during the march, Richard himself went out to Saphadin under a flag of truce. He offered to go home and leave the Muslims in peace if Saladin would evacuate the whole kingdom of Jerusalem. He cannot have expected that his proposal would be accepted, but perhaps that was merely a convenient way of publishing his maximum demand on the eve of a great battle that he hoped would be decisive.

The Battle of Arsuf, which took place just north of Jaffa on September 7, was, indeed, a Christian victory, but the Muslims were more frightened than hurt. To Saladin, however, it was a heavy blow. He ruled these men only because he led them to victory; if he made a habit of being beaten, as he had been beaten at Acre and Arsuf, they would find another sultan. Grimly, he prepared to make a stand in Jerusalem, for if he retired from that great conquest, his army would desert him.

Richard delayed in Jaffa to secure a base of operations to receive supplies from his fleet. Also, he had been talking with the knights of his army, and it suddenly must have been brought home to him that he could not win the war. Every pilgrim was eager to assault the Holy City, but every pilgrim would go home as soon as he had prayed in the Holy Sepulchre. Richard, in a position of strength following the victory at Arsuf, sat down to think out the best terms such strength would bring him.

He chose a good envoy: Humphrey of Toron, the brave, epicene warrior whose grandfather had bestowed on the youthful Saladin the girdle of knighthood. Humphrey spoke Arabic well, needing no interpreter, and he was known and liked by Saphadin.

To Saphadin, Humphrey advanced a reasonable compromise. Let Saladin retire from Jerusalem and the western half of the kingdom as far as the line of the Jordan, and the True Cross, of no value to

Saladin, should be returned. Saladin also had been thinking about what to do. The coastal plain was deadly, not only to himself but to his army; he began to see that he would never conquer the Christian ports. But in his answer to Richard, Saladin said that he would never yield Jerusalem. Though one day he might return the True Cross, the great prize must be dearly bought. Yet he still wished for peace. Could Richard make another offer?

Richard answered with a plan for the neutralization of the Holy Places, a plan quite unmedieval in its practical forethought. But since this was still the twelfth century, the foundation of the scheme was a royal marriage. Richard had with him in Jaffa his sister Joan, the widowed queen of Sicily. He offered to make over to her his conquests in Outremer, the strip of land he had conquered between Tyre on the north and Ashkelon to the south. Let Saladin give his brother the whole of Palestine, and then Joan should marry Saphadin. The plan was worked out in elaborate detail. The royal pair would reign in Jerusalem, which would be open to pilgrims of every faith; in each town would be separate Muslim and Christian quarters; all prisoners held by either side should be freed without ransom; the Templars and Hospitalers would return to their castles so that Christians would have armed protection.

As a scheme for the government of Palestine, the plan had great merits. In the proposed realm of King Saphadin and Queen Joan, Arab peasants, both Christian and Muslim, would till their fields in peace; Christian pilgrims would visit Jerusalem and go home again; in the ports, Italian traders would do business under an alien government, as in Alexandria and other Muslim markets. Turkish emirs and the knights of the military orders would keep the peace in open country.

But the plan was in advance of public opinion. When the Crusaders heard of it, they were shocked. Joan, furious, announced that she would never marry a Muslim. Then Richard asked Saphadin whether he would consider converting and got the expected answer.

To save his daring project, Richard offered his niece Eleanor of Brittany in place of Joan, but Saphadin would accept no substitute. The scheme was buried. Richard advanced to Beit Nuba, within twelve miles of Jerusalem, but changed his mind and marched south to Ashkelon. That decision gave him a valuable bargaining counter; a Christian army at Ashkelon could cut the road between Syria and Egypt, severing Saladin's recruiting ground from his principal source of revenue.

Therefore, at the end of March, Saladin, for the first time, made overtures for peace instead of waiting for Richard's envoys. Saphadin arrived with an offer: The Franks would have all the coast cities they had conquered, and in addition, the harbor of Beirut; they would enjoy free access to the Holy Sepulchre in Jerusalem, and as a bonus, the True Cross would be returned. For a fortnight, Saphadin was entertained as Richard's guest, and during the festivities, Richard knighted Saphadin's son. But the negotiations petered out.

Reports had reached Richard of his brother's constant encroachment in England. But before he could leave the Holy Land, he had to settle the rivalry between King Guy and Conrad. King Guy consented to abdicate, taking Cyprus as compensation; then Conrad, the unanimous choice of the barons, was murdered by assassins. Eventually, a compromise candidate was found, nephew to both King Richard and King Philip. When Henry of Champagne was proclaimed king of Jerusalem, Richard, at last, had the support of every Frank in Outremer. To cement his claim, Henry married Isabella, then twenty-one, seven days after her husband's death.

In June, Richard led his united army for the second time to Beit Nuba, only to learn that the wells between there and Jerusalem had been destroyed. His army could not live without water, so in July, he returned to Jaffa. From there, he sent envoys to Saladin; at last, the long negotiation seemed to be leading to a settlement.

If Richard would evacuate Ashkelon, Saladin offered not only peace but friendship with the new King Henry. The Franks might dwell undisturbed on the coast, and their priests could minister in the Holy

Places. Richard still argued, hoping to gain these terms and keep Ashkelon, too, but peace seemed so near that he moved north two weeks later to Acre, planning to embark for Europe.

Suddenly, Saladin swooped on weakly held Jaffa, marching down from Jerusalem in one day, July 27. Since Arsuf, in the previous September, he had been on the defensive, and Richard was taken unawares. Within three days, the Muslims breached the town wall, and the small garrison retreated to the castle. But Richard hastened to the rescue.

In the chapter of accidents that followed, Saladin was an eyewitness to the deeds of the Christian hero, though still the two leaders never met in a parley. Richard left Acre by sea while his army marched south by the coast road. When he was delayed by contrary winds, his army, not wishing to fight without him, loitered on the march. On July 31, he reached Jaffa, only to see Muslim banners on the town wall. He thought he had come too late, but a brave priest swam out from the beleaguered castle and explained the situation. Richard had with him only eighty dismounted knights, a handful of crossbows, and the Italian sailors of his ships. He waded ashore, and with this small force, drove the Muslims from Jaffa.

The next morning, Saladin sent his chamberlain to seek peace, still offering large concessions in return for Ashkelon. Abu Bekr found Richard joking with some captured emirs, explaining that Jaffa had been guaranteed to hold out for three months; Saladin had taken it in three days, and he, Richard, had won it back in three hours. He remarked that he had hurried so fast to the fight that he had charged still wearing his boating slippers.

Richard would not yield Ashkelon, but he offered to hold it as a fief under Saladin. This tactic might have worked if there had been a genuine peace: There was no compelling reason why Christian knights should not fight for Saladin against his Muslim enemies, but Saladin did not trust feudal tenures, and the offer was refused.

Richard and his escort encamped outside the walls of Jaffa, which was littered with unburied dead. The Muslims, while killing the unarmed citizens, also had killed all the pigs, and fragments of pork had been deliberately mingled with fragments of Christians, so burial was a slow process. The Frankish army had still not arrived when, on August 5, Saladin made a sudden assault on the unwalled bivouac.

Richard had about 2,000 men but only fifteen horses. With this force, he withstood the attack of 7,000 Turkish cavalry troops. In the afternoon, Saladin, watching from his usual post with the reserve, saw Richard counterattack. Then suddenly, the king of England was down, his horse killed under him. Overwhelmed by such a display of courage, Saladin made the noblest gesture of his life. Through the thick of battle, he sent a groom, leading two horses as a gift to his brave enemy. At the end of the day, the Muslims marched back in good order to Jerusalem.

Negotiations began again. The usual presents were exchanged. In the end, Richard agreed to evacuate Ashkelon after dismantling its fortifications. In return, Saladin promised five years of peace. Pilgrims would be welcome in Jerusalem, and Latin priests might serve in the Holy Places of Nazareth and Bethlehem as well as the Sepulchre. Most important of all, because Outremer needed the ships and trade of Italian merchants, Muslims would be free to trade with the Christian ports.

The treaty was signed on September 2. At once, a crowd of Western Crusaders visited the Sepulchre and then took the next ship home; Muslim emirs visited Jaffa to spend their pay on Western trinkets, and then returned to Saladin. That had been Richard's handicap from the beginning; his men would go home when they had fulfilled the pilgrimage, but Saladin's men were already at home.

Richard refused the humiliation of an unarmed visit to Jerusalem; on October 9, he embarked. Before leaving, he sent a last message to Saladin, boasting that when the five years of peace were over, he would come back to storm the Holy City. Saladin answered courteously that he would do his best to hold it, but that if God willed otherwise, Richard was the man most worthy to conquer it.

Saladin had retained his conquests at the cost of his life. He died on March 4, 1193, at the age of fifty-five, worn out by his exertions. His heirs were his seventeen sons, but by 1201, Saphadin, that experienced, cosmopolitan diplomat, had displaced them all and ruled over Syria and Egypt.

As king of England, Richard was a failure; only in Outremer did he show himself a statesman. His plan for a neutral kingdom of Jerusalem might have satisfied all parties if he could have persuaded his sister to marry a Muslim. He perceived that military victory was within his reach and that military victory would dissolve his army. Then he thought that Ashkelon would be a standing threat to Saladin. To the end, he bargained boldly and saved what could be saved - a thin strip ninety miles long and less than ten miles wide. But because he had given it an indispensable base in Cyprus, the kingdom of Jerusalem endured for another century. Of how many statesmen can it be said that their gains endure for 100 years? And besides his achievements as a diplomat and general, Richard was personally the best warrior in his army.

Saladin was no warrior, but he could recognize gallantry in others, and his gesture to Richard outside Jaffa is something in which both Christians and Muslims may take pride. In all these lengthy negotiations, neither was ever accused of double-dealing, neither broke his word. What is more, neither tried to convert the other. Today, as we watch the gyrations of those who wish to settle whole wars in one stroke, we should remember that long ago, two brave soldiers brought peace to a patch of land. Because they agreed to differ on essentials, they managed to reach a compromise. And for a few years, that was enough.

8

THE KNIGHTS TEMPLAR
MORRIS BISHOP

From modest beginnings, the Knights Templar became both
a military and then financial force to be reckoned with.
Their success didn't go unrecognized - or unpunished.

From modest beginnings, the Knights Templar became both a military and then financial force to be reckoned with. Their success didn't go unrecognized - or unpunished.

There once was a good man with a great idea. The great idea brought many to earthly joy and heavenly reward. But the great idea was corrupted, and those who espoused it were brought low, and their glory ended in screams and the stench of burning bodies.

The good man was Hugues de Payens, a knight of the Champagne country. He was pious, and he went out to the Holy Land, perhaps with the First Crusade around 1096. He was distressed by the plight of the pilgrims seeking to obtain divine grace and favor by visiting the Holy Places of Jerusalem. They landed mostly at Jaffa, modern Tel Aviv, and found the Promised Land without shade, water, or shelter - a mockery of promise. The forty-mile track to Jerusalem was beset by roving Bedouin brigands, and falling among thieves was a common experience on Palestinian roads.

Hugues de Payens proposed to create a volunteer escort to protect and assist the pilgrim bands from shipside to their goal. And this was his great idea - to enroll volunteers in a monastic order of men-at-arms, the Poor Knights of Christ. They should be drawn from the noble class, for only gentlemen were bred to fight. They should take the monastic vows of poverty, chastity, and obedience, but whereas proper monks were forbidden to shed blood, these new defenders of the faith should be ever ready with their swords. They would become the army of the Lord. "The soldier has his glory, the monk has peace," wrote historian Jules Michelet. "The Templar abdicated both. He accepted the heaviest burdens, the perils and abstinences, of both lives . . . The ideal of the crusade seemed realized in the Order of the Temple; it was the crusade fixed and permanent."

The idea of a military brotherhood under Church authority was not new. The Hospitalers, or Knights of Saint John of Jerusalem, had already been established to care for the sick and wounded crusaders and pilgrims, "God's poor," who were considered the representatives of Jesus Christ on earth. The Hospitalers, too, were gentlemen-at-arms, living under a monastic rule, but their main business was healing, not fighting.

The first Templars were a small nucleus of only eight or nine companions. Hugues de Payens went back to Europe and campaigned for funds and recruits. Meanwhile, Baldwin II, king of Jerusalem, found quarters for the order in his royal Temple, once the home of Solomon and Herod, today the Al-Aqsa mosque. Eventually, the Poor Knights of Christ were renamed the Templars.

At a church conclave in 1128, the great Abbot Bernard of Clairvaux, destined for sainthood, spoke eloquently for the Templars and wrote their charter.

It contained the surprising clause that the Templars should be responsible only to the pope, not to any political or ecclesiastical authority. Thus, they could defy kings and archbishops and fight or refrain from fighting only at the order of their Templar commander. The obligation of poverty was relaxed to apply only to personal property. The order, as a kind of corporation, might possess, administer, and solicit funds and property without limitation.

The charter specified the ranks of the brotherhood: the knights, who must be nobles by birth, the squires or orderlies, the attached chaplains, and the service troops. The behavior of all members of the order was strictly regulated: A knight was forbidden to look a woman in the face for more than a moment of recognition. The brethren had to sleep in lighted dormitories, wearing their breeches tightly laced. Doors must never be locked. Letters to individual members must be read aloud in the master's presence (not by the master, for he might well be unable to read). The regulation costume was a belted blouse or tunic bearing a red cross with each bar of equal length.

For informal wear, sheepskin breeches and jerkins were prescribed. The knights wore white; the squires, auxiliary troops, and technicians, black or brown. But all displayed the red cross, which became the symbol of aid to the suffering.

The Templars were toughened and drilled like commando troops for hand-to-hand fighting. They gained a reputation for ferocity in battle; indeed, brutality toward an infidel enemy was regarded as meritorious. The order attracted a certain type - brawny younger sons of the nobility and landless gentlemen doomed by poverty to bachelorhood; the illiterate; the unquestioningly devout; and those unconcerned about the mysteries of the faith but trustful of Christ's promises of salvation and confident in the efficacy of the sacraments. The military orders opened the religious life to soldiers whose trade - and whose joy - was killing.

Thus, the orders served the Palestinian states by providing a small but capable standing army at a time of severe manpower shortage. And to the disoriented young gentlemen in search of an honorable career, the orders offered tangible rewards - fulfillment of the knightly ideal, good fellowship, security and comfort for the survivors, and the certainty of salvation for those who should fall in defense of their Lord's Holy Sepulcher.

The ceremony of initiation is a straightforward warning of the hardships of Templar life and a demand that the initiate renounce all worldly concern, property, and ambition to conquer and defend the Holy Land. He must promise obedience to the master, and he must accept humiliation and degradation, feeding the pigs and performing kitchen chores for his soul's good. He might be ordered to eat his dinner on the floor among the dogs. His motto was: "*Fais ce que dois, advienne que pourra*" ("Do your duty, come what may.") In any peril, he was to repeat: "Living or dead, we belong to the Lord . . . Glorious be the victors, happy the martyrs!"

In their Jerusalem Temple and in their command posts here and there in Europe, the Templars followed a routine combining that of the convent and the army barracks. All, unless exhausted by military duties, were expected to attend matins, or services, at midnight. From the chapel, they proceeded to the stables to check on their horses and harness. Like most cavalrymen, they felt affection for their mounts. A visiting bishop, preaching to the Templars, said with an ill-placed sneer, "Truly he's a scoundrel who is more concerned with his horse than with Christ!" After a short sleep, the Templar was roused again at 4:00 a.m. for further prayer. Then again to the stables to repair equipment, drill, and do busywork like cutting tent pegs. Then an ample lunch, with two or three main dishes and plenty of wine. The order did not fast; it held that a Templar needed all his strength to wield sword, spear, and shield. The tableware was wooden, save for the master's metal drinking cup, which nullified poison. Silence was imposed during meals while the chaplain read from a holy book. If something was needed, one signaled according to the code of monks who vowed silence: For more bread, make a circle with the thumb and two fingers; for milk, suck the little finger; for fish, make a swimming motion with the hands; for crêpes, seize the hair with the fist.

The Templars of the East were rough-looking men, heavily bearded, lean from drill and battle, and deeply tanned from days spent under the fierce sun. Said Saint Bernard, "One never sees them with their hair combed, rarely with their faces washed. They stink of dust and are spotted with their harness and with heat." The chief offense of which the records accuse them is quarreling - inevitable among mettlesome youths used to fighting and living hard in a cruel climate.

The Templars had no special art of war beyond taking the offensive whenever possible. Their favorite device was the cavalry charge. More heavily armed and mounted than the Muslims, they terrified by their thundering onrush. But the enemy would not stand for the shock; his light horsemen would dash to within bowshot, send off a flight of arrows from horseback, and dash away. These tactics seemed unsporting to the French, encumbered as they were with armor, shields, heavy spears, and other weaponry.

The discomfort of steel armor in a Palestinian summer must have robbed death of much of its sting. A long tunic of chain mail could weigh fifty pounds or more. It would heat up like a fireless cooker. The occupant was not able to scratch, pursue a biting flea or louse, or wipe away a trickle of sweat. And if, perchance, he was afflicted - as many were - by dysentery, he had to half disrobe, with the aid of his squire.

Death in battle was the fate the brethren sought and gained. Hugues de Payens took out 300 volunteers from France; nearly everyone was dead within five years. Of the twenty-two grand masters of the order, five died in battle, five of battle wounds, and one starved himself to death in prison because he would not admit that any Muslim could be worthy of being exchanged for him. At the siege of Ashkelon in 1153, the Christians breached the wall; the Templar grand master admitted only men of his order "to have first choice of the booty," says a chronicler. The defenders killed those inside the walls, hanging them from the battlements. After the great Christian defeat at the Horns of Hattin in 1187, Sultan Saladin had all captured members of the military orders executed; they would be dangerous even in captivity. When the Khwarazmian Turks took Jerusalem in 1244 - putting a stop to Christian rule of the Holy City - the orders in the East were nearly wiped out. Only thirty-six Templars and twenty-six Hospitalers survived. The fighting orders needed - and received - constant replenishments from their homelands in the West.

Though the war of Christian and Muslim seems, in history's telescopic lens, to have been continuous, in fact, it yielded to long lulls of exhaustion or disinterest - but it smoldered, always ready to burst forth. After the first conquering rush, the Christians settled down in limited areas, and the Muslims thrust and withdrew and thrust again. The Templars were always in the thick of things, some dying gloriously, some not. The character of the perpetual war changed. The Christians no longer held the initiative; for lack of manpower, they had to keep on the defensive. They built castles to live in - enormous, indestructible, defiant buildings that still amaze the Western visitor. The Templars did their share, erecting thirteen mighty castles. Castle Pilgrim, or Château Pèlerin, with three sides standing in the Mediterranean, included pastures orchards, gardens, springs, fishponds, and a harbor with a small shipyard. Likewise, Saphet was an apparently impregnable self-supporting city, with a garrison of fifty knights and a thousand troops, mostly mercenaries.

The Templars, secure in their castles, often worked closely with Muslims on commercial and civic matters. Discussing police measures, mutual defense against common enemies from even farther east, land use, and water rights, the parties often became friends. As generation succeeded generation, a new caste of settlers appeared called *poulains*, or colts. These were born in the East of Armenian, Syrian Christian, or perhaps Muslim mothers. They were nursed in Arabic, sang and cursed in Arabic, and fed on Arab food. They dressed, by preference, in hooded cloaks. Though nominally Christian, they fraternized readily with the Muslims. There was even some osmotic filtering of culture. A few crusaders inquired into Buddhism, Confucianism, Hinduism, and Taoism. In 1274, the pope found it necessary to fulminate against apostate Templars.

Not many of the colts joined the military orders. Few of them could show sufficient nobility or muster sufficient zeal. But they certainly influenced the Templars, teaching them to treat the Holy Places with a merely respectful familiarity. A famous incident was recorded by a Muslim diplomat, Usama ibn Munqidh, during his visit to Jerusalem: "I entered the Mosque of El Aksa (sic). Beside it was a small mosque which the Franks had converted into a church. When I entered El Aksa, which was occupied by my friends the Templars, they assigned me to this small mosque for me to say my prayers. One day, I entered there and glorified Allah. I was in the midst of prayer when one of the Franks sprang upon me, seized me, and turned my face to the east, saying: 'I'll show you how to pray!' A group of Templars leaped upon him, grabbed him, and threw him out. I began my prayers again. But the same man gave the Templars the slip, sprang upon me again, and turned my face to the east, repeating: 'I'll show you how to pray!' The Templars jumped on him again and threw him out, then they apologized to me, saying: 'He's a foreigner who has just arrived from Frankland. He has never seen anyone pray without facing eastward.' I replied: 'I've done enough praying for today.'"

Naturally, Christian and Muslim alike inclined more toward a way of life than toward a way of death. Merchants of both faiths congregated on the coast, supplied the various armies, and built up the trade by camel caravan overland to the Far East. The Templars, almost inadvertently, became their bankers. They had several advantages to qualify them for this role. They possessed their Temple in Paris and extensive domains in Western countries, which were the gifts of grateful monarchs and pious donors. True, such gifts roused the jealousy of expectant and disappointed monasteries. Like proper churchmen, the Templars could promise the donor relief in purgatory, essentially spiritual tax deductions.

A European merchant or well-to-do pilgrim turned to the Templars as to a travel agency for aid and counsel. Funds in gold and silver were heavy, uncomfortable to carry, and provocative of thievery, but at a Templar preceptory, or command post, one could buy a draft on Jaffa or Jerusalem and depart in peace. Thus, the stores of gold and jewels tended to collect in the Western vaults of the order. In the East, also, the Templars offered the security of their castles for the deposit of funds. They employed their resources in loans to merchants and stranded pilgrims and eventually to princes and kings. Henry III of England stored his vast tax collections in their cellars. The Trésorier du Temple became the unofficial minister of finance for France. The papal chamberlain was usually a Templar. The order received fantastic presents - among them the city of Gaza, for instance, and the island of Cyprus. In short, the Order of Templars became very wealthy and powerful.

They also became arrogant and unpopular. The contemporary chronicler William of Tyre summed it up this way: "The brothers have become richer than kings . . . Their humility, guardian of all virtues, was succeeded by pride and greed."

They could still fight. When the stronghold of Acre fell, in 1291, to mark the end of the Christian state in the Middle East, the grand master and most of his men were wiped out. A new grand master, hastily chosen, sailed to Cyprus in an effort to raise men and money for a counterattack. But Cyprus would not budge, and the remaining Templars of the Holy Land made their way, mostly to France. They were ill-received. They had, after all, failed in their purpose, and the ending of the Crusades had ended their *raison d'être*. The public blamed them for the Crusades' failure, for uncountable deaths in an evil war, and for inflation, the devaluation of money, and hard times. In moments of depression, they must themselves have believed that Christ had played them false.

But they were still wealthy and powerful. Their center had shifted from Palestine to Paris where they made their home in the tall, terrifying ogre's castle that stood beside the present Square du Temple, near the Place de la République. The Templars' Villeneuve-du-Temple, a walled city with palace, bank, sanctuary chapels, and dungeons to secure gold or prisoners is said to have comprised a third of Paris. Here, the French crown was kept on safe deposit, and also for a time, the English crown jewels. From

Paris, the Templar properties radiated with branch offices throughout Europe. In France, the Templars handled much of the royal finances, collecting extraordinary taxes, such as those on fairs, Lombards, and Jews.

The king they served was Philip the Fair. He was unusually tall, with long, red-blond hair and a pale face. He was called the handsomest man in Christendom. A French bishop said of him, "If he looks at you silently, it is hard to sustain his glance. He seems no man or beast but a statue." He was commonly likened to a hawk. His icy arrogance bore down on all opponents, whether kings or popes. He thus addressed a letter to Pope Boniface VIII: "Philip, by the grace of God King of the French, to Boniface, alleged sovereign pontiff: no health at all, or very little. Let Your High Foolishness (*Vestra Insania*) be informed that . . ."

Philip treated the popes with regal contempt. When Boniface VIII dared defy him, Philip sent his chief aide, Guillaume de Nogaret, to Italy. Nogaret seized the aged pope, dressed in full pontifical robes, and slapped his face. Boniface died a month later. His successor, Benedict XI lasted only eight-and-a-half months. Rome was an unhealthy spot, particularly for popes. King Philip had much, if not everything, to do with choosing the next pope, a Frenchman, archbishop of Bordeaux, who took the name Clement V. He was a genial, kindly man of high principles and purpose. But he was sick - most likely from a stomach ulcer. And he was weak; he could not face Philip's reptilian stare.

Philip, always in need of money, hated the Templars, flaunting their wealth, their privileges, their power, and their accountability to the pope alone. Philip found it intolerable that so important a share of his lands and finances should lie under the control of a private, secret society. For years, he dreamed and schemed to transfer the Templars' property to his own hands.

There were several requisites to suppress the order and confiscate its wealth: a pliant pope; a favorable concurrence of circumstances, or simply a lucky chance; a public opinion conditioned to applaud the destruction of the order; an accusation that would submerge reason in horror. Today, the technique has come to be known as the Big Lie.

The lucky break came in 1303. A renegade Templar stabbed his commander and was jailed with another murderer, who may have been an informer. The Templar made his confession to his cellmate, recounting a string of blasphemies, denials of Christ, and ritual homosexual acts said to be practiced in the order. When the informant was released, he was rewarded by Guillaume de Nogaret, whose agents were busy infiltrating the Temple and spreading rumors about unholy deeds occurring within it.

Four years later came another favorable occurrence. Pope Clement, dreaming of a new Crusade, summoned the grand masters of the Templars and the Hospitalers from Cyprus to France. The Hospitaler declined to participate; the grand master of the Templars, Jacques de Molay, accepted. That was a mistake. He appeared in Paris in 1307, with a princely escort including twelve horses allegedly laden with gold and silver. That was another mistake.

Jacques de Molay, now about sixty, had spent his life in the order. Himself illiterate, he was the leader of an anti-intellectual party; he confiscated all books found in his knights' possession. He was devoted to the welfare of the Templars but was apparently not very intelligent. He distrusted what he did not possess - cleverness. He visited Pope Clement in Poitiers and begged that the current rumors about Templar misconduct be properly investigated and the conclusions published. The pope put off a decision, and the king seized the initiative. On October 12, 1307, he assigned Molay the task of holding a corner of his sister-in-law's funeral canopy. And the next day, October 13, Black Friday, at dawn, every administrator, bailiff, and high official in France broke the seal on a top-secret message and proceeded to jail Jacques de Molay and all accessible Templars, whether knight or subordinate, in total about 13,000. This mass arrest was in defiance of the pope, who was not informed of the action in advance.

The charges against the Templars were published for the world to read. They were, in summary, that the Templars set the welfare of their order above every religious and moral duty; that they were in secret collusion with the Muslims; that initiates were required to spit on the crucifix and deny Christ; that any member venturing to reveal the order's secrets was assassinated; that Templars despised the sacraments and had revised the Church's teachings to suit their abominable purposes; that they encouraged homosexual practices and imposed shameful kisses, even as a part of the initiation; that they betrayed the Holy Land; that they worshiped the devil in the form of a cat or of various grotesque images.

Since the Templars were churchmen, they could be tried only in ecclesiastical courts. The pope became sick - no doubt his ulcers were in a fury - but he authorized the trial and ordered the Inquisition to collect evidence. The grand inquisitor was King Philip's chaplain, and courts of the Inquisition were set up throughout France.

Apparently, many of the accused began with indignant denials of the charges. Then the inquisitors used the cunning and cruelty of interrogators everywhere, the "empty stomach and full bladder," alternations of mood from kindness to threats, the offering and withdrawal of promises, exhaustion of the accused until he could not recall what he had said or recognize what he was signing. After this, the victim who had refused any admission was turned over to the torturers, gleeful sadists chosen for their ingenuity in inflicting and prolonging pain. Enough that, according to a Templar priest who was present at the Paris Inquisition, thirty-six brothers out of thirty-eight died under torture, their deaths reported as suicides. "I would have confessed to murdering God," said one Templar who survived. Another excused his confession by saying, "I can't plead all alone against the pope and the king of France."

They confessed to anything the inquisitor suggested. Having once confessed, they were guilty but accessible to pardon. If, however, they retracted their confessions, they would be relapsed heretics and therefore unpardonable. Instead of meeting a quick death by hanging, they would be burned alive.

No positive evidence of heresy was found in the search of the Templars' quarters, no obscene idols or blasphemous texts. The pope fought feebly for reason and mercy. In 1309, he proclaimed a pontifical *enquête*, or inquiry. This chiefly elicited the refusal of the prisoners to sustain the confessions made under torture. When two years later, the Templars seemed to be gaining popular sympathy, Philip managed the appointment of a favorite as archbishop of Sens and charged him with settling the fate of the prisoners. The archbishop staged a show trial. His commission sped its work and announced the penalties. Fifty-four defendants who had retracted their confessions were designated relapsed heretics and were turned over to the secular arm. On May 12, 1310, they sang while being burned to death. When the fires cooled, a crowd pressed forward to gather the possibly wonder-working ashes.

But the fires still smoldered. Outside France, trials were staged, but they ended in acquittals (as was the case in Portugal) or in mild condemnations. After two years of agitation and recrimination, the pope succeeded in declaring the Order of the Temple suppressed and transferred its property to the Knights Hospitaler. In France, Philip the Fair, by a brilliant exercise of accounting, was able to appropriate most of the Templars' lands and goods.

Some of the Templars were pardoned; some escaped and went underground. A few of the leaders were spared temporarily. Jacques de Molay, summoned before a commission of cardinals on March 18, 1314, found courage enough to declare, before heaven and earth, that he had committed the worst of crimes in admitting the accusations against the order. "I attest, and truth obliges me to attest, that the order is innocent. I said the opposite only to suspend the excessive pains of torture, to influence my tormentors. I know the tortures inflicted on the knights who have had the courage to retract their confessions; but my dreadful previsions cannot make me confirm a first lie by a second. In the infamous conditions imposed on me I gladly renounce my life."

On the following day, Molay and a fellow recanter were burned on a tiny island in the Seine, now buried under Pont-Neuf. Citizens swam to the islet to collect miracle-working fragments. In a way, they were justified. The Masonic order named for Molay has 15,000 members in the United States and Canada. That is a kind of wonder in itself.

Molay was burned on March 19, 1314. A month later, Pope Clement died, perhaps of cancer. In November, Philip the Fair died of a stroke or a heart attack while hunting. In the same year, Guillaume de Nogaret and three accusers of the Templars also died. People said, of course, that Molay had summoned all of them to stand trial at that supreme court from which there is no appeal.

In 2007, the Vatican published documents about the trial indicating that Clement had absolved the Knights of the charges of heresy. The document, known as the Chinon Parchment, was written in 1308 and had been misplaced in the Vatican archives. While clearing the order of heresy, it nevertheless recognized some level of immorality, and it was Pope Clement's intent to reform the Knights. But under pressure from Philip, Clement never carried out his plan.

The Templars soon disappeared, their work undone. For a long time, the story was told that on every Black Friday, October 13, a specter, fully armed and wearing the white mantle with cross, would appear in the ruins of the Paris Temple. He would cry, "Who will deliver the Holy Sepulcher?" The vault of the chapel would reply, "No one. The Temple is destroyed!"

9

THE TROUBADOURS
FREDERIC V. GRUNFELD

The joyful, often bawdy, music of Provence changed forever
our notion of romantic love. But brutal repression
during the Inquisition led to thousands of deaths
and the burning of 500 towns.

The joyful, often bawdy, music of Provence changed forever our notion of romantic love. But brutal repression during the Inquisition led to thousands of deaths and the burning of 500 towns.

Some aspects of the scene may seem vaguely familiar: scores of long-haired young men roaming the country with stringed instruments under their arms, singing songs that proclaim a sexual revolution, that are both urbane and immensely influential songs, and that catapult some of their authors into the ranks of the rich and famous. But the time is the twelfth century, the place is southern France, and the young men in question are known as *troubadours*, which is to say "composers," since the verb *trobar* (to find, to invent) covers all manner of poetic and musical invention.

If the word troubadour has a faintly off-putting sound to our modern ears, that is because it was so heavily abused in the nineteenth century; somehow we find it hard to rid ourselves of the tedious image of the fat tenor *trovatore* in tights and tassels, singing and strumming his lute while a chaste lady listens at a tower window. Nothing could be further from the actual troubadours, who were more like the Rolling Stones than grand opera in their methods and their way of looking at the world. Singing of love, sex, and politics, they were the underground press of their day - and the above ground press, too, since there was virtually no other way of disseminating news.

On the literary landscape, they appear like crocuses in the snow after the long, hard winter of the Middle Ages. If the troubadours are here, can Dante and the Renaissance be far behind? They come, too, as apostles of an epicurean style of love that brings new depth and balance to the relationship between the sexes. Sometimes they are even given credit for having invented romantic love, though that seems to be stretching a point. What they did discover, certainly, is the idea of love as an art to be cultivated, a pleasure to be prolonged and intensified by, among other things, music and poetry.

The philosophers of classical antiquity had maintained that love was a sort of madness to be got over as quickly as possible. In addition, its higher forms were reserved for men only. The fathers of the Christian church equated physical love with mortal sin and indicted woman as the great corrupter. "Every woman ought to be overwhelmed with shame at the thought that she is a woman," wrote Clement of Alexandria. It was the troubadours of Mediterranean France - a land of nightingales singing in the soft light - who first introduced an air of elegance into the rather brutish mating habits of the Middle Ages. They turned love into a condition of civilization and vice versa. Along with their southern neighbors, the sensualist love-poets of Moorish Spain, they came to see woman not as "the gate of hell" but as the great provider of pleasure and inspiration. "I'll surely die of longing and desire," sings the troubadour Bernart de Ventadorn, "if that beauty does not call me near her, there where she lies, to let me caress and kiss her, and press against her white, soft, smooth body." (The translation is from Anthony Bonner's *A Troubadour Anthology*, the first to be published in English. Other translations from this collection will be marked with an asterisk.)

Since their sentiments were too intimate, too passionate to be expressed in monkish Latin, the troubadours became the first poets in history to create a literature in a modern European language. In doing so, they launched the great woman-centered lyrical tradition that still dominates our poetry. Their language was that form of medieval Romance language later known as Provençal, though it extended far beyond the boundaries of present-day Provence. At its peak, Provençal was spoken in fully a third of the territory comprising modern France; its influence extended north as far as Britain and south as far as Sicily, Majorca, and Spain. Along with Arabic, it was the literary language par excellence.

Provençal is not a dialect but an independent language - rich, easy to sing, supple in its vowels and yet hard-edged in its consonants, with a lithe, melodic lilt. All the great Provençal poets are masters of onomatopoeia, the formation of words from their sounds. Maurice Valency, the Columbia professor who wrote a book on the psychology of the troubadours, *In Praise of Love*, was fascinated by the unity of sound and idea in their poetry. "When the mood is smooth, the verse is smooth; grief, anger, despair are matched with corresponding sounds, rough, sharp, grave, dark, shrill. In the instrumentation of the mood, every sort of rhetorical device was pressed into service - internal rhymes, displaced rhymes, broken stanzas, puns and alliterative tricks, sound-effects of all sorts, sometimes amazing in their virtuosity, sometimes annoying, but seldom boring."

Ezra Pound loved the troubadours for their fireworks and recklessness; they were great takers of chances, verbal or otherwise, and like himself, totally committed to a life of provocation. When they came riding out of their hilltop fortresses twanging their lutes and fiddling with their viols, they risked their lives on the open highway not because this was the only career open to a communicator in the Middle Ages but "for love of the fair time and soft, and because fine love calls me to it" (as Gaubertz de Poicebot wrote and Pound translated).

This message of love is usually expressed as a declaration of intent and anticipation not unlike the Beatles formula, "I Want to Hold Your Hand." Arnaut Daniel, for example, prays to the Lord to let him lie with his lady so that he might experience "the great joy of having her, amid kisses and laughter, disclose her fair body that I may gaze at it beneath the lamplight." Bernart de Ventadorn hopes that his mistress will have the courage "to have me come one night there where she undresses, and make me a necklace of her arms." Count Guilhem of Poitiers, who reigned from about 1086 to 1127 and ranks as the first of the troubadours, expresses the hope that God will let him "live long enough to have my hands beneath her cloak," and he boasts in verse that he can make love eighty-eight times in a week. Marcabru, another of the early poets, has a remarkably modern song in which he says, "I will die unless I know whether she sleeps dressed or in the nude." Bertran de Born describes the mistress of his heart - and the twelfth century's ideal woman - as a lady "delicate and fair, charming, gay and young; her hair is blond with a ruby tint, her body as white as hawthorne, with soft arms and firm breasts and a rabbit's suppleness in her back." Cercamon, Marcabru's teacher, claims that he cannot endure life "unless I have her next to me, naked, to kiss and embrace within a curtained room."

Many of these objects of affection were married, of course, and their husbands were condemned to play - at least in verse - an ambiguous and unenviable part in the ritual of fine love. As a matter of good form, the troubadour usually addressed his love songs to another man's wife, and the husband was supposed to regard this as an honor to his house. Unmarried women were out of it altogether (except shepherdesses, whom in pastoral poems were always invited to share haystacks), and no one sang of love to his own wife. It was taken for granted that marriages were contracted for practical reasons, and one had best look for love outside the home, preferably at the feet of some high-spirited and well-connected lady with a taste for poetry, like Eleanor of Aquitaine. If, as in Eleanor's case, the lady herself was skilled at composition, she could reply in kind. Beatrice, Countess of Die, the most gifted poetess of the epoch, wrote her love songs not, of course, for her husband but (it is said) for the troubadour knight Raimbaut d'Orange:

How I would like to hold him

one night in my naked arms

and see him joyfully use my body

as a pillow . . .

My handsome friend, gracious and charming,

when will I hold you in my power?

Oh that I might lie with you

one night and kiss you lovingly!

For the lady's husband to become actively jealous was considered both silly and dishonorable, a breach of the spirit of courtesy. Yet the record suggests that this was a fairly common occurrence and one of the occupational hazards of being a troubadour.

The rules and requisites of courtly love were all duly set down in a manual entitled *Flos amoris*, or *Ars amatoria*, produced by Andreas Capellanus (Andrew the Chaplain) about 1200. His system was complex and represented an effort to bring a certain order to the anarchies of the flesh. Among his thirty-one rules of conduct were the following:

1. Marriage cannot be pleaded as an excuse for refusing to love.

2. A person who is not jealous cannot love.

3. None can love two at once. There is no reason, however, why a woman should not be loved by two men, or a man by two women.

4. It is love's way always to increase or lessen.

14. Easy winning makes love despicable; the difficult is held dear.

20. The lover is always fearful.

28. A slight presumption in the lover awakens the co-lover's suspicion.

It was no more than an elaborate charade, but it worked for well over a century because the troubadours managed to make it interesting. "There was unspeakable boredom in the castles," Pound wrote. "The chivalric singing was devised to lighten the boredom." They sang, talked, and argued interminably about the fine points of courtly love, often in rhymed dialogue-debates known as *tensons*.

The lord of a castle could consider himself fortunate when the troubadours came to his great hall to sing the praises of his wife. Aside from the sheer entertainment value, it was a matter of prestige and public relations, for songs had enormous currency in a world without newspapers. The Limousin troubadour Gaucelm Faidit, for instance, extolled the beauty of Jordana d'Ebreun so effectively that "no valiant man of Vienne or of all Provence thought himself worth a straw unless he had seen her." This sort of social asset could work to her husband's advantage when it came time to forge alliances.

From the troubadour's viewpoint, the ideal patron was someone like Blacatz, Lord of Aups, who had a formidable reputation both as a poet and as a supporter of other poets. "And he delighted in ladies, and love, and war, and spending, and feasting, and tumult, and music, and song, and play, and all such things as give a good man worth and fame. Never was there a man who loved better to take than he to give . . ."

Money was scarce, and the great nobles rewarded their poets with payment-in-kind: horses, armor, or feudal privileges. Perdigon, a fisherman's son who could play and sing and write poetry was knighted by the Dauphin d'Auvergne and received "land and revenues."

For a fisherman's son to be knighted as a poet was a remarkable occurrence. Theoretically, the troubadour poet was supposed to be a knight, but in practice – despite the two dozen reigning princes whose names are on the list - he tended to come from the middle or low classes. It was as democratic and egalitarian an institution as anything the Middle Ages could produce. The many *vidas,* or troubadour biographies, that have come down to us in manuscript present an astonishingly broad cross-section of feudal society. Bernart de Ventador was the son of a castle servant "who gathered brushwood for the heating of the oven wherein was baked the castle's bread." Marcab was a foundling left on a rich man's doorstep in Gascony. Elias Cair was trained as a goldsmith. Raimbaut de Vaqueiras was the son of a poor Provençal knight "who passed for mad." Folquet de Marseille was the son of a Genoese businessman; Guilhem Figueira a tailor's son from Toulouse, and Peire Vidal the son of a furrier. Arnault de Marvo was "a clerk of low birth who, because he could not earn his bread by letters, took to wandering through the world, and well knew to sing and rhyme." Gaubertz de Poicebot became a monk as a boy and then "for desire of woman he went forth from the monastery."

Many of the most important troubadours began their careers as jongleurs, professional entertainers singing other people's songs, and then went on to become recognized composers in their own right. The distinction between a jongleur and a troubadour was social as well as occupational. The jongleur figured in the company of clowns, mountebanks, and tightrope walkers; he was a lineal descendant of the classical Roman *joculatores* (jesters). Though he might specialize in singing and playing instruments, he was well advised to cultivate more than one string to his viol. "I can sing a song well," a medieval minstrel could boast, "and make tales to please young ladies and can play the gallant for them if necessary. I can throw knives into the air and catch them without cutting my fingers. I can do dodges with string, most extraordinary and amusing. I can balance chairs and make tables dance. I can throw somersaults and walk on my head."

Like composers of a later day, established troubadours often relied on the professionals to sing their works in public. Jongleurs were apt to have better voices and what we now call stage presence. We hear of Rigaut de Barbezieux, for example, that although he was an excellent knight at arms who cut a handsome figure, he "was very fearful of singing before people, and the more good people he saw the more confused he became and the less he remembered." Giraut de Bornelh seems to have spent his winters teaching and composing, and his summers going from court to court "taking with him two jongleurs who sang his songs." As usual, however, there were not enough good voices to meet the demand. "It worries me," said Giraut, "when some hoarse-voiced jongleur, who's not been properly paid, recites badly and thus spoils my lofty songs."

The vocal reviews in the *vidas* and in the poems that troubadours wrote about each other could be unmerciful. A thirteenth-century music critic writes of

Peire de Valeria: "His singing was of no great worth nor was he." Peire d'Auvergne, the son of a tradesman in Clermont-Ferrand, runs down a long list of his colleagues and finds that none of them can sing. There is Guilhem de Ribas, of the hoarse voice, whose "stutterings" are worthless. There is Giraut de Bornelh, who reminds Peire of an oyster dried in the sun, "with his pitiful, meager singing like that of some old woman water-carrier." There is the man they call the Limousin from Brive, who sounds "like some sick pilgrim." As for Peire himself, he tells us that his own voice "is like a frog singing in a well," but adds without false modesty: "yet he compliments himself in front of everyone, for he's master of them all."

Verses of this sort, which have nothing to do with love, belong to the category known as *sirventes* and come under the general heading of news and public affairs. Politics, personalities, the arts and fashions, and all the scandals of the day were grist for the mill of the *sirventes*; their purpose was humorous, instructive or critical. Some are protest songs about social injustice: "If a poor man robs a bedsheet, he's called a thief and bows his head, but if a rich man robs a treasure, he is honored in the court . . . If some beggar robs a bridle, he'll be hung by a man who's robbed a horse."

During the Aquitanian battles between Henry II and his sons, the task of stirring up the local barons fell to the troubadour Bertran de Born, Viscount of

Hautefort in Perigord and one of the great warmongering poets of the epoch. Bertran was an immensely clever manipulator of *sirventes* as a propaganda weapon; he was said to be capable of writing "such a song as will shatter a thousand shields, pierce and smash helmets, hauberks, doublets and actons." If the scribes are to be believed, "he always wanted the kings of France and England to be at war with each other. And if there was a peace or truce, he would try by means of his *sirventes* to undo it, and prove how each had been dishonored by this peace." Apparently, he loved war both for its own sake, the way an actor loves the theater, and because the small barons stood to gain as long as the great lords were preoccupied with the struggle for power. He writes glowingly about the "joyful season" of war when knights appear on the scene, catapults are fired, and fields are strewn with bodies. To Bertran, war was the logical climax of political life:

I love to see the press of shields

with their hues of red and blue

of ensigns and of banners

many-colored in the wind,

and the sight of tents and rich pavilions pitched,

lances shattered, shields pierced, shining

helmets split, and blows exchanged in battle.

As long as these campaigns were conducted on a reasonably friendly footing, they brought no intolerable hardship to the people who dwelled in the shadow of the castles. But early in the thirteenth century, the full disasters of war overtook the land of the troubadours, and poets learned to sing a more doleful tune. Using religious heresy as a pretext for invasion, the north of France launched a "crusade" against the south that all but eradicated the basis of Provençal civilization.

At Béziers, a town of 40,000, every living thing was put to the sword. "Kill, kill! God will know his own," was the notorious order issued by the Abbot of Citeaux when the French soldiers discovered that they could not distinguish between true believers and heretics. At Carcassonne, the jongleurs stood on the walls playing their instruments and hurling defiance at the besieging armies, but the city surrendered after its leaders were seized. Five hundred towns and castles were stormed, sacked, and cleansed of heresy by fire. As always, the news traveled with the troubadours. "Ah, Toulouse and Provence and the Land of Argence, Béziers and Carcassonne, such I but late knew you and such do I behold you now!" sings Bernard de Marjevois. "The world is put to confusion; the bonds of law are broken; the troth of oaths is fouled." Peire Cardenal, a knight's son who himself had been trained for the clergy at the Canonry of Le Puy, composed a series of angry *sirventes* against the invading Frenchmen who came in the name of God.

"Churchmen pass for shepherds, but they're murderers," he declared. "Kings and emperors, dukes, counts and viscounts, and knights as well used to rule the world; but now I see churchmen holding sway with their thefts and treachery and their hypocrisy, their violence and their preaching."

Though the crusaders were ultimately withdrawn, Provence was formally annexed to northern France, and its culture ceased to exist as a separate entity. Troubadour poetry after the fall became stylized and moralistic; the *cansos* that poets formerly composed for their mistresses were now readdressed to the church or to the Virgin. In 1229, the Council of Toulouse established the Inquisition as a regular tribunal, bringing to an end what British publisher Ford Madox Ford calls "the last civilized state and creed that Europe was to know."

Several unreconstructed troubadours found refuge in Lombardy and in Sicily, where their example prompted Dante Alighieri to try his hand at poetry in the Italian vernacular and "to put into verse things difficult to think."

Meanwhile, the last of the great troubadour poets, Guiraut Riquier, emigrated from his native Narbonne to the court of Alfonso the Wise of Castile. He was a gifted poet, but the times were against him.

Riquier would write: "Song should express joy, but sorrow oppresses me, and I have come into the world too late." He died about 1294, and with him, so did the living tradition of the troubadours. There remained about 2,500 poems preserved in various manuscript collections and some 270 examples of their music, written in a rudimentary notation that provides no more than the melodic outline of each song. So, we still know only half of their achievement, for as Folquet de Marseille said in one of his songs, "A verse without music is a mill without water."

The songs that have survived were set down not by their composers but by other hands, working from aural tradition and with the only forms of notation available at that time.

It seemed to me that we would have to give up hope of ever knowing how troubadour music sounded. But one day, on the sun-drenched plains of Majorca, I heard an old man singing a folk song as he was knocking almonds out of a tree with a long pole, and suddenly it was clear to me how the troubadours sang their songs - with a taut, irregular rhythm that expands and contracts with the inflections of the language and a vocal line ornamented with Moorish arabesques, like smoke rising and curling on a breeze.

As it happens, these Majorcan folk songs have hardly changed since the fateful year 1229, which marked not only the end of liberty in Provence but also the invasion of Majorca by a force of Catalans under Jaime I of Aragon, who was at the same time lord of

Roussillon and Montpellier in southern France. Jaime - a great patron of troubadour poetry - pushed the Moors out of Majorca and settled his own followers on the island. Their language was first cousin to the Provençal spoken by the troubadours.

It is not an accident that Majorcan peasants refer to their songs as *vers*, just as the early troubadours did, and that they employ some of the same images and rhyme schemes as those that occur in twelfth-century troubadour songs. If you go into the remote corners of the island, perhaps you can still hear echoes of the *cansos* that Bernart de Ventadorn sang to Eleanor of Aquitaine and the love letters that the Countess of Die sent to Raimbaut d'Orange. They are the remnants of a far-distant earthquake, of the sexual revolution of the Middle Ages.

For when a young girl works in the olive orchard pruning trees, she sings:

And I stand on a hill

in the crown of an olive tree

high on the hill.

And here in the heights

I can truly pray,

for a lover, and

for a painless fall

if I should tumble from my branch

high on the hill . . .

And you can tell Miguel

that when he comes to see me

I shall belong to him,

I shall belong to him.

10

ALFONSO THE
LEARNED OF CASTILE
FREDERIC V. GRUNFELD

A renaissance man in the Middle Ages, he marshaled
the talents of Christians, Jews, and Muslims in an
extraordinary outpouring of scholarship and art.

A renaissance man in the Middle Ages, he marshaled the talents of Christians, Jews, and Muslims in an extraordinary outpouring of scholarship and art.

"He has such a passion for knowledge that all the good, learned men who go to him are well contented," wrote the troubadour Girault Riquier about Alfonso X, the thirteenth-century king of Castile who was to go down in history as Alfonso *El Sabio* ("The Learned"). Most of the other poet-composers who frequented his court were equally enthusiastic about the treatment they received there. Folquet de Lunel rhymed and sang of it as "*a Cort ses erguelh e cort ses vilania*" - "a court without pride or villainy, in which no good man's hopes for reward are disappointed, a court without constraints or oppression, in which one listens to reason, a court where there are a hundred givers of rewards" - i.e., the arts were subsidized.

Alfonso's domain extended well beyond the boundaries of Castile itself, for he was also king of León, Galicia, Seville, Córdoba, Murcia, Jaén, and the Algarve, which meant that he ruled over the greater part of Spain from the Bay of Biscay in the north to the Guadalquivir in the south, and over a polyglot population that spoke Portuguese-Galician and Arabic as well as several dialects of Castilian. His southern provinces had been wrested from the Moors only a few years before his accession to the throne in 1252: Seville, his favorite capital, and some of the other ex-Islamic towns still preserved their superb

Moorish architecture - notably the great castles, like the Alcazar of Seville, and the mosques, like the Great Mosque of Córdoba, which the Christians had simply redecorated and converted into churches. A no less useful legacy were the Arabic books that had survived the wars and the tradition of scholarship and literature that had accounted for the glories of Andalusian civilization under the preceding centuries of Muslim rule.

Culturally, Alfonso's kingdom straddled East and West, and (unlike his more fanatical successors, who tried to uproot everything that was non-Christian in Spain) Alfonso decided to make the best of both worlds. His court became a meeting place for Christian, Islamic, and Jewish scholarship and art, as well as a refuge for the last of the troubadour poets fleeing the south of France in the aftermath of the Albigensian Crusade.

Alfonso's lifelong interest in secularizing culture made him the first Renaissance Man of the Middle Ages: One of his senior scholars, Jehuda ben Moses Cohen, describes him as a king "in whom God has placed intelligence, and understanding and knowledge above all the princes of his time." His task, as he saw it, was to mobilize the intellectual energies of Spain; he commissioned the leading scholars of the day to produce an imposing array of books on history, law, astronomy, magic, mythology, and games. He was not a royal dilettante and usually took a direct hand in the production of these manuscripts, either as contributing author or as royal editor in chief. His literary method is described in a passage of his *General Estoria*: "The king writes a book, not in the sense that he writes it with his own hand, but in the sense that he gathers the material for it, amends, edits, and corrects it, shows the manner in which it should be presented, and orders what is to be written; and for this reason we say that the king writes the book."

Alfonso's astronomers were responsible for the compilation of planetary movements (based on Arabic models) known as the "Alfonsine Tables," which, in subsequent editions, were to be essential to navigation through the time of Columbus; their appearance in 1272 signaled the dawn of European science. As a lawgiver, Alfonso codified the *Siete Partidas* in which Roman law was reconciled to the ancient regional laws and customs of Spain. His chronicle of Spain ranks as the first history of a European nation, other than the Anglo-Saxon, to be written in a modern European language. His book on chess is the first European work of its kind and also the most beautiful ever produced.

But the most astonishing of all his books are the superbly illustrated manuscripts of the *Cantigas de Santa Maria* - the royal collection of poems in praise of the Virgin, which is one of the great art treasures of the Middle Ages. If ever a work of art held up a mirror to its time, it is this vast compendium of music and poetry and pictures, now preserved in the library of El Escorial Palace near Madrid. The four surviving *Cantigas* are illuminated with over 1,300 miniatures in various stages of completion; they document virtually every aspect of life in thirteenth-century Spain, from architecture and warfare to medicine and sexual relations. Using a frame-by-frame narrative technique that anticipates the comic strip, the artists of Alfonso's court created a sort of time capsule that preserves the very essence of an age that has been called the "most fascinating and excellent moment of man's creative history."

Here the whole pageant of medieval humanity passes in review: Cloth merchants sail to England to buy wool; foreign pilgrims brave the dangers of the long road to Santiago de Compostela; Moorish horsemen are arrayed against the Christian cavalry; jongleurs fiddle and sing for the great lords in their castles. Day-to-day life in the towns and villages of Spain is depicted with an astonishing wealth and variety of detail: We meet the apothecary, the innkeeper, the greengrocer, and the moneylender; people play stickball and watch bullfights; peasants plow their fields and ride to market in an oxcart; a farmer's family sits up with a sick mule in the stable; women give birth and nurse their infants, gamblers brawl in taverns, prostitutes ply their trade in the streets, monks prepare feasts in their refectories, *caballeros* go hawking and hunting, a queen is carried in a sedan chair. The medical department includes physicians dispensing drugs, nurses bandaging the wounded, an operation for the removal of an arrow from a soldier's head, the amputation of a diseased foot, several cases of dementia, a fever epidemic, leprosy, a monk evidently suffering from delirium tremens, and a hospital scene where patients, seven to a bed, are treated in a clinic founded by a humanitarian (a rare figure indeed in Alfonso's *Cantigas*) who tenderly nurses the poor "and gives to all, bread and wine and meat and fish."

Some of the other scenarios involve naval engagements, and we see battle scenes with renderings of weapons and armor; shipwrecks, drownings, robbers and rapists attacking wayfarers, murder in the cathedral; the pursuit of cattle rustlers, criminals of all kinds being arrested and punished. We see them flogged, hanged, decapitated, stoned, speared, dragged through the streets, and burned at the stake.

The sexual situations depicted in the *Cantigas* might have been chosen by Ingmar Bergman: A young girl who has vowed to preserve her chastity is sexually assaulted by her bridegroom and his accomplices; a woman loses her husband and sleeps with her own son; when they have a child she kills it by throwing it down a toilet (bathroom fixtures are, of course, included among the architectural details).

A knight seduces a nun and abducts her from the convent. A prioress has to undress before a bishop to prove she is not pregnant. A monk cannot break the habit of making love to women, "both married ones and unmarried ones, nor did he leave virgins alone, nor nuns, nor sisters of charity." A black man sleeps with a white woman; both are arrested in bed at her mother-in-law's instigation and condemned to the stake, but Santa Maria intervenes to save the white woman.

All of these stories are narrated and illustrated with complete candor; it was an age without our elaborate notions about what is unmentionable. Nor was it strange that these sensual and sinful activities should appear in a book of religious songs. At the crucial moment (and usually at the eleventh hour), the Madonna dispenses justice and mercy or resolves the problem with a miracle. Some of these are simply household miracles, of course, as in the story of the peasant from Segovia "who lived in a village and lost a cow he loved very much."

The peasant prayed to Santa Maria to bring back his cow, vowing to give her its first offspring in repayment: "And the cow came back, unharmed and unhurt, with its ears hanging low." Eventually, it bore a bull calf, and the peasant, forgetting his vow, took the calf to market. But it got away and went into a church to pay homage to the Madonna. From then on "there was not a better work bull in the village," and its owner became a very pious man. In some of the other domestic cantigas, the intercession of the Virgin is not so much miraculous as merely therapeutic. One of the songs, for example, tells about the troubles of a merchant's wife whose husband is out "enjoying himself with his *barragana*" (harlot), but in due course, after the wife has prayed to the Virgin, the other woman sees the error of her ways, makes friends with the wife, and allows the married couple to be reconciled.

There are 423 cantigas that have been preserved with their music, all of them written in the Galician dialect that is much closer to Portuguese than Castilian and that was the preferred poetic idiom of thirteenth-century Spain. It's not clear what Alfonso's role was in the writing of the *Cantigas*. Certainly, he played an editorial role in all of them, and he must have composed a considerable number himself, judging from the texts that bear a distinctive personal touch. In some of them, he recounts his experiences in the first person:

Porén uos direr o que passou per mí

iazend' en Bitoira enfermo, assí

que todos citudauan que morress' alí

et non atendian de mí bon solaz. . . .

With this I shall tell you what happened to me

When lying ill at Vittoria, and

Everyone believed I would die there,

And did not expect me to recover. . . .

And he goes on to relate how refusing the remedies

prescribed by physicians, he asked that the book of the *Cantigas* be placed on his body, and the cure was immediate. He was indeed a man with an extraordinary faith in the power of the written word.

The cantigas were written for solo voice and were to be accompanied by one or perhaps up to three instruments. It was the troubadours and jongleurs of the court who performed not only Alfonso's religious works but also the worldly songs that are ascribed to him, notably the curious "cursing-out" songs known as *cantigas de maldizer*, in which he denounces his enemies, and the *cantigas de amor*, with their bawdy folk humor about the possibilities and impossibilities of love. When love songs were performed, the singers were usually women, but in the miniatures of the *Cantigas de Santa Maria*, only male singers are represented.

The range of instruments shown in these illuminated manuscripts is incredible: One of them illustrates more than fifty different types of instruments available to a great court with a well-stocked music room. Christian, Moorish, and Jewish musicians play trumpets and horns, large and small lutes, vielles both plucked and bowed, gitterns, rebecs, psalteries, mandolas, organistra (hurdy-gurdies), chime bells, drums, cymbals, castanets, tabors and tabor pipes, bagpipes, recorders, flutes, shawms and double-shawms (two primitive oboes whose mouthpieces are tied together), and a great many other varieties no longer on the active list. Their function was not to play together to produce a pattern of harmonies (that intriguing idea had not yet appeared on the musical horizon) but to play in pairs or small groups to mark the rhythm of a dance or to support the solo voice.

Many of these instruments had first come to Spain with the Moors. The lute, for example, derives from the Arabic al-'ud, "the wood." Seville had been the musical center of Moorish Spain prior to its capture by Alfonso's father, Fernando III, in 1248, and its craftsmen had long been renowned for their musical instruments. During the Moorish epoch, the rulers of Andalusia had been in the habit of importing singers, poets, and books from the ancient centers of Persian culture. Students from all parts of the Islamic world had flocked to Seville to learn singing, and to Córdoba to study science and theology. Under the liberal-minded caliph, al-Hakam II, the library of Córdoba is reported to have contained approximately 400,000 volumes.

The Moorish era in Spain has been compared to a great torch bringing light into a world of darkness. Certainly a cultural gap did exist, and the disparity is best illustrated by the two kinds of architecture erected by the Moors and the Christians in their respective corners of the peninsula - on the one hand, the heavy, windowless structures of the Romanesque style, stamped with the siege mentality of the Middle Ages; on the other, the airy, elegant lines of Moorish architecture, with its soaring columns and lacy arches, its screens and courtyards and audience chambers. It was no wonder that this culture became the envy of Europe and that, despite the intermittent warfare between the two sides, the Christian kings, such as Alfonso, felt obliged to match the Moorish emirs in music and literature.

But there was always more than one string to Alfonso's lyre, and his vast range of scholarly interests took him far beyond religion and into problem areas that were afterward to be condemned as heretical. (His father, Fernando *El Santo*, was canonized by Pope Clement X for his orthodoxy, but sainthood for Alfonso was conspicuously unforthcoming.) Some of the early chronicles state that Alfonso had both the Koran and the Talmud translated into Castilian, but no traces of these have been found - perhaps because they were destroyed later during the Inquisition. For his part, Alfonso had tried to keep such intolerance in check. In 1255, he established an independent secular legislation on religious matters, which removed his kingdom from all papal interference. One heretical work that did survive is the *Book of Muhammad's Ladder*, or *Livre de l'eschiele Mahomet*, which he had translated from the Arabic into Castilian, and thence into French. It deals with the Prophet's ascent through the seven astronomical heavens of the Ptolemaic system, led by the Angel Gabriel, until he reaches the throne of God; later, still with Gabriel as his guide, he learns of the sevenfold division of hell and its monsters and torments.

The resemblance to the *Divine Comedy* is evident, and it has been suggested that Dante may have seen a copy of this translation - or that he may have discovered the same legend by some other route.

Most of Alfonso's technical and scientific books also derive from Arabic or Persian sources. The *Libros del saber de astronomía (Books of Astronomical Knowledge)* include Jehuda ben Moses Cohen's translation of a catalogue of the stars by "Abderrahman the Sufi," and five books on various kinds of timekeeping mechanisms (sun, water, clockwork, candle) by Rabbi Isaac ibn Sid and Samuel ha-Levi, as well as treatises on the "round astrolabe" and "flat astrolabe" of Rabbi Isaac. The *Libro de las formas (Book of Star-Judging)* and *Libro de las cruces (Book of Crosses)* are astrological works adapted from various Arabic authorities, and there are four *Lapidarios* that deal with the scientific, medical, and magical properties of 360 different stones.

But the most fascinating of these Moorish-inspired reference works is the *Libro de los juegos*, another of Alfonso's magnificently illuminated manuscripts, and the first great chess treatise of Europe. It contains instructional diagrams for some 150 games, mainly of chess but also of dice and backgammon. The 100-odd chess problems - "Black mates White in five moves," and so on - not only illustrate the position of the pieces on the board but also portray the players. A black Moorish king may play against a white Christian king; ladies are pitted against gentlemen of the court (one of the first recorded instances in medieval Europe of true sexual equality, at least with respect to board games); Arabian lords are shown in their resplendent costumes, and Alfonso himself is depicted playing against one of the women of his court. The book also explains how to play chess in combination with dice, and how to set up the four-cornered "chess of the four seasons" and the *grant acedrex* ("great chess") of India, played on a board with twelve squares in each row and twenty-four pieces to a side. There is even a seven-sided game of "chess which one plays with astronomy," in which the pieces symbolize the planetary system. Evidently, chess was one of Alfonso's great passions, and in the introduction, he goes to great lengths to explain that "God has intended men to enjoy themselves with many games," and that these include not only jousting, fencing, and such, but also "sitting games" like chess, which can be played by night as well as by day: "Even women who do not go riding and who stay at home can take pleasure in them, as well as old or weak men, or those who like to enjoy themselves in private to avoid the annoyance and unpleasantness of public places, or those who have fallen into another's power, either in prison, or slavery, or as seafarers, and in general all those who have time on their hands because they have no opportunity to ride, or hunt, or go anywhere, and are obliged to stay at home, and are looking for a pleasant pastime which will bring them comfort and dispel their ennui. And for that reason, I, Don Alfonso . . . have commanded this book to be written."

This is the tone of a man accustomed to command, and to cover all possible legal contingencies as he does so. We know that he always took a keen interest in the style of the books produced under his patronage: There is a note in one of the astronomy volumes to the effect that "the king corrected it and ordered it to be written, and he deleted the materials that he thought superfluous and redundant and not in correct Castilian, and he added others that he thought appropriate; and, as to the language, he corrected it himself."

What makes all this even more remarkable is that Alfonso and his committee of scholars were the first people to write Castilian prose: They were in the curious position of codifying their own language in the course of systematizing what they knew about the world. While Latin continued to be used for such purposes in the rest of Europe (and he himself went on writing poetry in Galician), Alfonso deliberately established Castilian as the official language of the kingdom; it was to become one of the few unifying factors in Spanish history.

The books that did most to establish Alfonso as "the father of Castilian prose" are the two great chronicles, the *Estoria de España* and the *General Estoria*, for which "I, Don Alfonso . . . gathered many writings and many histories of ancient facts, and chose from amongst them the best and most truthful I could find, and from them I had this book made, and I ordered that all the facts I chose should be included." They contain very little original material. The *General History* breaks off at the birth of Christ, and the *History of Spain* is compiled from earlier chronicles, Arabic accounts, and even some epic poetry. What does emerge from Alfonso's description of Spain is a sense of his personal vision of this realm being "like a paradise of God" - a fertile land of great mineral wealth and natural abundance, "foremost among nations in ingenuity, bold and powerful in war . . . and with a great love of learning."

That, in essence, was Alfonso's ambition for his kingdom, and at every opportunity, he tried to expand its intellectual resources. One of his first concerns after inheriting the crown was to establish a university at Seville, and at the same time he strengthened the university at Salamanca - where, among other things, he decreed that music should henceforth be included in the curriculum: "There shall be a *maestro de organo* [i.e., a teacher of theory and composition] to whom I shall give fifty maravedis a year." His comprehensive legal code, the *Siete Partidas*, includes the first Spanish laws concerning universities, and again he is very specific about the privileges he wants them to enjoy: "The town in which a university is to be established should have good air and beautiful environs, so that the professors who teach the sciences, and the students who learn them, can live healthily and sleep pleasantly in the afternoon, when they have become fatigued by their studies. . . There should also be an abundance of bread and wine, and of good inns in which they can live and pass their time, without great cost. We also declare that the citizens of the town in which the university is established should protect and honor the teachers and scholars, and all of their belongings. And the messengers who come to them from their home towns should not be arrested or interfered with, even if their parents happen to be in debt."

Alfonso stipulated that students and teachers had the right to form corporations and to elect their own rectors. Students were prohibited from carrying arms and from bribing the examiners; they were entitled to quiet places for study, and to lending libraries where they could rent their textbooks. It was an educational code far ahead of its time.

If intellectual achievement counted in political life, Alfonso would have been the most successful of monarchs. In fact, he was nothing of the kind. His reign was marked by economic and political disasters. One chronicler wrote, "He studied the heavens and watched the stars, while losing the earth and his kingdom." Through his mother, Beatrice of Swabia, he had inherited a claim to represent the Hohenstaufen line, and in 1257, he was actually named emperor by four of the seven Electors of the Holy Roman Empire. But the election was declared invalid, and Alfonso never managed to have his title recognized by the popes. The result was that he spent a great deal of Spanish money pursuing his European ambitions, was obliged to raise taxes and debase the coinage, lost the support of his nobles and the middle classes, and lived to see his own son take the field against him in a civil war.

Of all his domains, only Seville remained loyal to him. Before his death at sixty-three, in 1284, he was reduced to trying to pawn his crown jewels in order to pay the army. It was as though he had fallen victim to that peculiar fate that Spanish destiny reserved for intellectual excellence of any kind - the ironic and persistent twist of the Spanish tale that had Columbus imprisoned after discovering a new world, Cervantes living in dire poverty, Goya dying in exile, and Lorca shot in an olive grove. "Affliction has fallen on me," Alfonso wrote to a cousin, shortly before his death. "All men will know my misfortune and its sharpness, which I suffer unjustly from my son, my friends, and my prelates. Instead of making peace, they have done wrong - not in secret or disguise but with bold openness. I find no protection within mine own land, neither defender nor champion. I have not deserved thus. . ."

11

THE BLACK DEATH
PHILIP ZIEGLER

It came out of Central Asia, killing one-third of the European
population. And among the survivors, a new skepticism
arose about life and God and human authority.

It came out of Central Asia, killing one-third of the European population. And among the survivors, a new skepticism arose about life and God and human authority.

In 1346, a Tatar army picked a quarrel with Genoese merchants who traded in the Crimea, chased them into their coastal redoubt at Feodosia, and laid siege to the town. The usual campaign of attrition was developing when the plans of the attackers were disastrously disrupted by the onslaught of a new and fearful plague. The Tatars abandoned the siege, but not without first sharing their misfortune with their enemies. They used their giant catapults to lob the corpses of the victims over the walls, thus spreading the disease within the city. Though the Genoese carried the rotting bodies through the town and dropped them into the sea, the plague was soon as active within as it was without. Those fortunate inhabitants who did not immediately succumb knew that even if they managed to survive the plague, they would be too weak to withstand a renewed Tatar attack. They escaped to their galleys and fled toward the Mediterranean. With them traveled the Black Death. Within three years, every third man, woman, and child in Europe was dead.

The Black Death was bubonic plague, endemic to certain remote areas of the world. From time to time, it erupts in minor, localized epidemics. Far more rarely, it surges forth as a great pandemic. Unlike influenza, bubonic plague moves slowly, taking ten years or more to run its course. The high mortality rate of its initial impact is followed by a long period of occasional flare-ups that gradually die away in frequency and violence. Finally, perhaps several centuries after the original outbreak, the plague vanishes.

Three such pandemics have been recorded. The first, beginning in Arabia, reached Egypt in 542. It ravaged the Roman Empire of Justinian and moved on across Europe to England, where it was known as the Plague of Cadwalader's Time. The second was that of the Black Death, which died out in the seventeenth century. One of its parting flourishes was the Great Plague of London in 1665. Finally came the pandemic that started in 1892 in Yunnan and reached Bombay in 1896. In India, it is believed to have killed some 6 million people. It moved briefly into Suffolk in 1910, finding only a handful of victims.

Though it is impossible to be categorical about the origins of the medieval pandemic, investigations near Issyk-Kul, a lake in central Asia, show that there was an abnormally high death rate in 1338 and 1339. Memorial stones attribute the deaths to plague. Since this area is in the heart of one of the zones in which bubonic plague lies endemic, it is likely that this was the cradle of the Black Death. From there it spread eastward into China, south to India, and west to the Crimea some eight years later.

In this part of central Asia, the bacillus *Pasteurella pestis* has lingered on, living either in the bloodstream of an animal or the stomach of a flea, typically *Xenopsylla cheopis*, an insect that usually resides on the hair of some rodent. We will never know for certain what ecological upset began the migration: It could have been flooding, drought, or a sudden increase in the rodent population that strained the available supply of food. Whatever the cause, there is little doubt that infected rats, fleeing from Asia, carried the plague with them to Europe.

The symptoms of bubonic plague as known today coincide precisely with those described by medieval chroniclers.

The bubo, an inflammatory swelling of a lymph gland, is the classic sign. Sometimes the size of an almond, sometimes of an orange, it is found in the groin, the armpit, or occasionally on the neck. Equally familiar are the dusky stains or blotches caused by subcutaneous hemorrhaging and the poisoning of the nervous system.

A variant form of the plague, known as primary pneumonic or pulmonary, was even more lethal. In the epidemics of the late nineteenth century, between 60 and 90 percent of those who caught bubonic plague died. In the case of pneumonic plague, which attacks the lungs, recovery was virtually unknown. Pneumonic plague also killed more quickly and is perhaps the most infectious of epidemic diseases.

The fourteenth-century plague is unique because in its drive across Europe, it changed from pneumonic to bubonic with the seasons of the year. The medieval doctor can hardly be blamed for finding the process incomprehensible. Even if he had understood it, he would not have mastered the full story. For there were also cases in which a man would die within a few hours of falling sick or go to bed in the best of health and never wake up.

A third form, septicemic plague, was also present at this time. Like bubonic plague, it is transmitted by insects. The brunt of the infection falls on the blood stream, which, within an hour or two, is swarming with plague bacilli. The victim is dead long before buboes have formed. In this variety of plague, a man-borne flea, *Pulex irritans*, has a chance to operate. So rich in bacilli is the blood of a sick man that the flea can easily become infected and carry the disease to a new victim. Septicemic plague must have been the rarest of the three interwoven diseases that made up the Black Death, but it was certainly as lethal as its pneumonic cousin.

The population that awaited the Black Death in Europe was

ill-equipped to resist it. The medieval peasant - distracted by war, weakened by malnutrition, exhausted by his struggle to farm increasingly unproductive land - was physically an easy prey for the disease.

Intellectually and emotionally, he was prepared for disaster and ready to accept it.

The Europeans of the fourteenth century were convinced that the plague was an affliction laid on them by the Almighty, a retribution for the wickedness of their generation. Credulous and superstitious, they believed without question in the direct participation of God on earth and were well versed in Old Testament precedents for the destruction of cities or entire races. Because they were unable to see a natural explanation of this sudden onset of disease, they assumed they were the victims of God's wrath.

Given so grim a sense of destiny, it is to the credit of the medieval physicians that they devoted themselves to preventing or curing the infection. But it is hardly surprising that their efforts proved inadequate. Medical historian Karl Sudhoff's archives, published in Germany in 1925, included more than 280 plague treatises, seventy-seven written before 1400 and at least twenty before 1353. While many amount to windy nothingness, common sense and sound judgment are also evident. Even though there was a depressing readiness to stress flight or prayer as the only possible defense, the patient was also given some guidance on how to conduct himself.

There were frequent differences of opinion among the experts. Simon of Covino thought pregnant women and "those of fragile nature," like undernourished paupers, would be the first to go. By contrast, the Medical Faculty of Paris said that those "whose bodies are replete with humors" were the most vulnerable. There was more agreement on the best place to live. Seclusion was the first priority. After that, the problem was how to avoid the infected air. A low site, sheltered from the wind, was desirable. The coast was to be shunned because of the corrupt mists that crept across the sea. Houses should be built facing north, and windows should be glazed or covered with waxed cloth.

If the infection was carried by corrupted air, something was needed to build up antibodies. Anything aromatic was considered of value. For example, it was good to burn dry and richly scented woods, like juniper, ash, vine, or rosemary. Diet was important, too. Fish from the infected waters of the sea were prohibited, but eggs were authorized if eaten with vinegar.

It was bad to sleep by day and best to keep the heat of the liver steady by sleeping first on the right side and then on the left. To sleep on one's back was disastrous.

Bad drove out bad, and to imbibe foul odors was a useful protection. According to another contemporary writer, John Colle: "Attendants who take care of latrines are nearly all to be considered immune." It was not unknown for apprehensive citizens to spend hours each day crouched over a latrine absorbing the fetid smells.

These were mainly preventives; once the disease struck, the remedies became still more irrelevant. Bleeding was a part of almost every treatment: If the patient fainted, wrote one physician, pour cold water over him and continue as before. Various potions were prescribed, in particular, a blend of apple syrup, lemon, rose water, and peppermint. There was some belief in the virtues of emeralds and pearls, and the medicinal qualities of gold were taken for granted. One recipe instructed: take an ounce of best gold, add eleven ounces of quicksilver, dissolve by slow heat, let the quicksilver escape, add forty-seven ounces of water of borage, keep airtight for three days over a fire, and drink until cured, or, as was more probable, death supervened. At least the high price of gold ensured that not many invalids could be thus poisoned.

Most fourteenth-century people regarded their doctor with tolerance and respect but also with an uncomfortable conviction that he was irrelevant to the real problems of their lives. They were, of course, ready to believe almost anything stated with authority, but their faith had been considerably undermined by the doctor's own lack of confidence.

The Black Death arrived in Messina, Sicily, early in October 1347. Within a few days, the plague had taken a firm grasp. Too late to save themselves, the citizens turned on the sailors who had brought this disastrous cargo and drove them from the port. With their departure, the Black Death was scattered around the Mediterranean, but it was too late for Messina. With hundreds of victims dying every day, the population panicked. They fled from their doomed city into the fields of southern Sicily, seeking safety in isolation and carrying the plague with them through the countryside.

From Sicily, the plague spread probably to North Africa by way of Tunis; certainly to Corsica and Sardinia; to the Balearics and Almería, Barcelona, Valencia, and on the Iberian Peninsula; and across the narrow channel that separates Sicily from southern Italy. The disease closely followed the main trade routes: Whether the Black Death traveled by rat, unescorted flea, or infected sailor, a ship was the surest means, and its first targets were the coastal towns. It traveled from the Crimea to Moscow, not overland, but by way of Italy, France, England, and the Hanseatic ports.

The three great centers for the propagation of the plague in southern Europe were Sicily, Genoa, and Venice. It seems to have arrived at the latter ports sometime in January 1348. But a few weeks later, it was Pisa that provided the main point of entry to central and northern Italy. From there, it moved inland to Rome and Tuscany. It had begun the march that would not end until the whole of the European continent had been blanketed by death.

France was the next country to be overrun. The plague arrived at Marseilles a month or two after it reached the mainland of Italy. Through 1348, it moved across the country, advancing on two main lines, toward Bordeaux in the west and Paris in the north. The fate of Perpignan, just north of the Spanish border, illustrates vividly what happened in many of the smaller cities. The disruption of everyday commercial life is shown by statistics of loans made by the Jews of Perpignan to their Christian co-citizens. In January 1348, there were sixteen such loans, in February, twenty-five, in March, thirty-two. There were eight in the first eleven days of April, three in the rest of the month, and then no more until August 12. Of 125 scribes and legists known to have been active shortly before the Black Death, only forty-five survived. Physicians fared even worse - only one out of eight survived - while sixteen out of eighteen barber-surgeons perished or, at least, disappeared. In Avignon, then the papal capital, Pope Clement VI retreated to his chamber, saw nobody, and spent day and night sheltering between two enormous fires. He survived, but the poet Petrarch's beloved Laura died in the same town.

Two of the Black Death's most unpleasant byproducts emerged in Germany. The first was the Flagellant movement. The Brotherhood of the Flagellants, or Brethren of the Cross, as the movement was called in 1348, traditionally originated in Eastern Europe, but it was in Germany that it really took root, and it was the Black Death that turned the whim of a freakish minority into a powerful international force. The

Flagellants marched in long processions, two by two. Men and women were segregated, the women taking their place toward the rear. At the head was the group master. Except for occasional hymns the marchers were silent, their heads and faces hidden in cowls, their eyes fixed on the ground. They were dressed in somber clothes with red crosses on the back and front.

At the news that the Brethren of the Cross were on the way, the townsfolk would pour out to welcome them. The first move was to the church, where they would chant their special litany. The real business, however, usually took place outside. A circle was formed, and the worshipers stripped to the waist. Their outer garments were piled inside the circle, and the sick of the village would congregate there in the hope of acquiring a little vicarious merit.

First, the master thrashed those who had committed offenses against the order, then came the collective flagellation. Each brother carried a heavy scourge with three or four leather thongs tipped with metal studs. They began rhythmically to beat their backs and breasts. Three of the brethren, acting as cheerleaders, led the ceremonies. The worshipers kept up the tempo and their spirits by chanting the hymn of the Flagellants. The pace grew. Each man tried to outdo his neighbor, literally whipping himself into a frenzy. Around them the townsfolk quaked, sobbed, and groaned in sympathy.

Eventually, the movement was taken over by a small

group who used their power to bully and blackmail the local inhabitants. One can understand and forgive much because of the panic that impelled these misguided fanatics, but it is impossible to condone the impulse they gave to the second byproduct of the Black Death, the persecution of the Jews.

It was perhaps inevitable that a people overwhelmed by fear and suffering should seek revenge. The Jews were not the only candidates. In Spain the Arabs, in France the English, in England the lepers - all were at one time suspected of spreading the plague. But there were also economic reasons for wanting the Jews out of the way, and these, allied with traditional anti-Semitism, ripened into a ferocious conviction that the Jews were poisoning the wells. The first cases occurred in the south of France, but the madness might never have spread if, at a trial at Chillon in September 1348, lurid confessions of guilt had not been racked from certain of the accused. This settled the doubts or perhaps quieted the consciences of many who might otherwise have felt bound to protect the Jews. The municipality of Zurich voted never to admit them to the city again. In Basel, the Jews were penned up in wooden buildings and burned alive.

"In November began the persecution of the Jews," wrote a German chronicler. In that month, Jews were burned at Solothurn, Zofingen, and Stuttgart; in December at Landsberg, Burren, Memmingen, Lindau; in January at Fribourg and Ulm. Gotha and

Dresden followed, and at Speyer, bodies of the murdered were piled in great wine casks and sent float-
ing down the Rhine. A lull of a few months ended
in fresh outbreaks extending to Spain and Flanders.
The persecution of the Jews waned only with the
plague itself.

That the persecution of the Jews did not accompany
the Black Death to England owes less to tolerance
than to the fact that almost all of them had already
been expelled. The first cases of the plague probably
occurred at Melcombe Regis, in Dorset, in June or
July of 1348. By the end of 1349, the British Isles had
been blanketed.

England is peculiarly rich in archives that illustrate
vividly and in detail the life of the past. The ecclesiastical books of institutions and patent rolls, the memorial court rolls and account rolls provide material
to plot the course of the Black Death with greater
authority than elsewhere in Europe. Inevitably we
know most about the clergy. It might be supposed
that their education, high standard of living, and less
cramped living quarters would give the clergy a better chance of survival than their unfortunate flocks.
But their death rate was higher. Their work, if con-
scientiously carried out, brought them into constant
contact with the infected; their average age was relatively high; their smaller households, though less
easily infected, were more vulnerable once penetrat-
ed. By some estimates, the norm was one rat family
to a household and three fleas to a rat; the greater

the number of infected fleas in proportion to potential human victims, the smaller were the chances of escape.

What is certain is that the clergy suffered hideously. It is extraordinary to note when visiting medieval churches how often the incumbent was replaced once, twice, or even three times during the plague. In Bristol, for example, ten out of eighteen clergymen died. Not that the laity did much better. Thirty percent of the fifty-two council members in Bristol died in 1349. Things were far worse in the crowded and stinking warrens in which the poor were forced to live. "The plague," according to an old calendar, "raged to such a degree that the living were scarce able to bury the dead."

The Black Death reached London early in 1349. The existing graveyards were soon too small to meet the demand. A new cemetery was opened at Smithfield, while the distinguished soldier and courtier Sir Walter de Manny bought some thirteen acres of unused land to the northwest of the city at Spittle Croft. He built a chapel, dedicated to the Annunciation, and threw it open for the overflow of victims. The London historian John Stow recorded an inscription in the churchyard that read: "A great plague raging in the year of our Lord 1349, this churchyard was consecrated; wherein, and within the bounds of the present monastery, were buried more than fifty thousand bodies of the dead . . . whose souls God have mercy upon. Amen."

A figure of 50,000 for a city of 60,000 to 70,000 inhabitants seems unlikely. Statistics for the big cities are particularly hard to establish, but it seems more probable that between 20,000 and 30,000 died - a sufficiently terrifying figure to satisfy even the most bloodthirsty chronicler.

Yet the mark left by the Black Death was not only seen in the cemeteries. The sharp fall in moral standards, noticed in so many parts of Europe at this period, was nowhere more striking than in London. Criminals flocked into the city, and chroniclers tell of the great increase in lawbreaking. After this period, the city began to enjoy a dubious reputation for wealth and for wickedness. Thomas Walsingham denounced the Londoners roundly: "They were of all people the most proud, arrogant and greedy, disbelieving in God, disbelieving in ancient custom." Those who live in great cities are traditionally thought to be harder, more sophisticated, and more rapacious than their country cousins, but the Londoner probably deserved his reputation. Yet a city that suffered as London did and rebounded rapidly to even greater prosperity could perhaps be excused a certain fall from grace during the years of its recovery.

In London, perhaps 30,000 out of 70,000 died. Was this true of England as a whole, of France and Italy? Statistics are always hazardous, in the Middle Ages particularly so. All one can do is extrapolate from the small pockets of certain knowledge - the lists of beneficed clergy, court rolls for certain manors, post-mortems - and venture an educated guess. The statement that a third of the population of Europe died of the Black Death should not be considered too misleading. Modern estimates suggest the death rate could have exceeded 40 or even 50 percent.

The death of so many people created considerable dislocation to Europe's economy and social structure.

It is unquestioned that, in England at least, the Black Death did not so much introduce radical changes as vastly accelerate changes already going on. England had already begun to move from the manorial system to a new relationship in which land was rented and services paid for in cash. The sudden disappearance of so much of the labor force meant that those who already worked for wages were able to demand an increase, while the rest clamored to share in the freemen's privilege. If the landlord refused, conditions were favorable for the tenant farmer to slip away and seek a more amenable master elsewhere. As successive waves of the pandemic broke over the countryside, the balance between tenant and landlord swung still further. Wages in many areas more or less doubled; prices temporarily fell; labor grew more mobile. Inevitably there was a backlash. Though the genesis of the Peasant's Revolt of 1381 may be found far earlier, it was the Black Death that ultimately created the conditions for rebellion.

The pattern of centuries was breaking up; not only the pattern of society but of men's minds as well. Any account of the Black Death that ignored its impact on the minds of its victims would be incomplete. Its effects endured. Within only a few years, the horrors of the plague were no longer at the forefront of people's minds, but certainly, no one can live through a catastrophe so devastating without retaining psychic scars.

People felt, fairly or unfairly, that the Church had let them down. It had failed to protect its flock, had forfeited its claim to special status. On the whole, the best of the churchmen perished; those who shirked their duty - and perhaps didn't attend to the sick with diligence - survived to preach again. In 1351, Pope Clement VI accused his clergy of arrogance, covetousness, and licentious living: In so doing, he spoke for the majority of humankind.

The decades that followed the plague saw not only a decline in the spiritual authority of the Church but also a growth of religious fervor. There was a spate of church building throughout Europe. In Italy, nearly fifty religious holidays were created. The number of pilgrims to Rome and other centers remained constant or increased, even though a third of those who might have made the journey were now dead. The second half of the fourteenth century was marked by resentment at the wealth and complacency of the Church and by fundamental questioning of its philosophy and its organization. In England, it was the age of theologian John Wycliffe and of Lollardry, a new and aggressive anticlericalism. In Italy, it was the great period of the Fraticelli, or "Little Brethren," dissident Franciscans who believed that poverty was the essence of Christ. The second half of the fourteenth century was a time of spiritual unrest, of disrespect for established idols and a search for strange gods. In the end, the Reformation would have happened anyway, but the tempo would have been slower, the opposition more intense, and the reaction more immoderate.

"Faith disappeared, or was transformed: men became at once sceptical and intolerant," wrote the French scholar and diplomat J. J. Jusserand in 1889. "It is not at all the modern, serenely cold, and imperturbable scepticism; it is a violent movement of the whole nature which feels itself impelled to burn what it adores; but the man is uncertain in his doubt, and his burst of laughter stuns him; he has passed, as it were, through an orgy, and when the white light of the morning comes he will have an attack of despair, profound anguish with tears and perhaps a vow of pilgrimage and a conspicuous conversion."

This classic description of the European in the second half of the fourteenth century captures the twin elements of skepticism and timorous uncertainty. The generation that survived the plague could not believe but did not dare deny. It groped toward the future, with one nervous eye always peering over its shoulder toward the past.

225